Sooner
Sunset

Janet Lee Barton

To my family for loving me and supporting me always.
To JoAnne Simmons for helping make
this series the best it could be.
To those strong men and women
who settled in the state of Oklahoma.
And to my Lord and Savior for showing me the way.

A note from the Author:
I love to hear from my readers! You may correspond with me by writing:

Janet Lee Barton
Author Relations
PO Box 721
Uhrichsville, OH 44683

ISBN 978-1-61626-589-2

eBook Editions:
Adobe Digital Edition (.epub) 978-1-60742-706-3
Kindle and MobiPocket Edition (.prc) 978-1-60742-707-0

SOONER SUNSET

All scripture quotations are taken from the King James Version of the Bible.

This book is a work of fiction. Names, characters, places, and incidents are either products of the author's imagination or used fictitiously.

Our mission is to publish and distribute inspirational products offering exceptional value and biblical encouragement to the masses.

PRINTED IN THE U.S.A.

one

Charity Logan believed her life to be the least boring of any of her friends or family. She spent most weekends in the city and the rest of the time in Guthrie. And she loved both places. But her loyalties were with her hometown. Especially since Governor Haskell had called for a special election in June to decide whether the capital of Oklahoma would remain in Guthrie or be moved to Oklahoma City. Oh, there were times when she wished the capital, and all the politics that went with it, were somewhere else. She got sick of the constant headline fighting between the two leading newspapers in town—the *State Capitol* and the *Daily Leader*. But what would happen to her hometown and her family, if—

She shook her head and forced her thoughts away from what might be. It would do no good to worry, and the day was too pretty to waste one more minute doing so. The redbuds were in bloom, their pinky-violet color standing out against the green leaves of oak and sweet gum. The near-to-bursting buds on those trees that hadn't quite come into bloom yet lent an almost-green hue to them, and Charity imagined tiny leaves trying to force themselves into full bloom. Clumps of wildflowers were beginning to show their color along the roadside, and prairie grasses changed direction with the gentle wind. Spring was definitely in the air.

A light breeze fanned her face as she steered her red touring auto down the road from Oklahoma City to Guthrie. She'd had the car only a few months—since her nineteenth birthday—and she loved driving it. As she bounced along the road, she enjoyed the simple freedom of traveling alone.

She smiled, thinking about how long it took for her to persuade her father to let her make the drive by herself. For the first month, he'd insisted on riding with her, going to Guthrie with her on Monday mornings after she'd spent a weekend in Oklahoma City. Then he'd take the auto back with him to Oklahoma City until the next Friday, when he'd come back to get her and let her drive into the city under his supervision once more. Finally she'd convinced him she knew what she was doing, and he'd allowed her to make the trip alone. But he'd made her promise to telephone as soon as she got to the boardinghouse where she stayed in Guthrie while working as a bookkeeper and designer apprentice at his office there. She'd been sketching her own home plans for years and hoped to be able to head her father's business one day.

She loved working for Logan Building and Design and was proud of what her father had accomplished with his company. Over the years, it had expanded to Oklahoma City, where he and Charity's mother had moved a few years ago. As long as she could see them most weekends, she was perfectly happy staying at the boardinghouse her father had built for her mother before they were married. She'd been born in that house, and it would always be home to her. Rose, her adopted grandmother, still lived there along with Charity's cousin Hope and her family.

Midway between Edmond Station and Guthrie, she passed her Uncle Ben's farm and could see the top of the two-story house her father had designed and built for him. Fruit trees of all kinds—apple, peach, pear, and even cherry—were beginning to bloom. She looked forward to the weekend when she'd be on her way back to the city. They might even be in full bloom by then. Her uncle had made quite a name for Thompson Farms, buying up land around him and making sure he only delivered the best quality fruit and vegetables to his vendors. Why, he even shipped to the city and up into Kansas now.

Charity passed a farm wagon heading out of Guthrie, but she hadn't encountered much traffic on this Monday morning. Most people probably made their way into town earlier in the day—not everyone worked for a parent who'd rather have breakfast with his employee than have them arrive to work on time. She truly was spoiled. But she did the best job she could when she got to Guthrie, wanting to help her father in any way she could. He'd worked so hard to get where he was now and—

Charity caught her breath as something that looked like a fox bounded out into the road ahead and stopped. And stayed there. She quickly pulled on the brake as hard as she could. But before she could register she'd come to a stop, she heard the crunch of metal and felt a thud at the back of her vehicle. The impact threw her forward and knocked the breath right out of her.

❧

Luke Johnson drove down the highway, his mind full of a dozen different angles to write about the governor's decision to hold a special election on moving the capital. But the sound of a braking auto just ahead of him jerked him out of his thoughts. He yanked on the brake as fast as he could, but it was too late. As he heard the crush of metal hitting metal, he pitched forward from the sudden stop.

"Must be a woman driver," he muttered under his breath as he unwound his legs to step out of his roadster. He rubbed his chest, which throbbed from hitting the steering wheel, and went to inspect the damage. Finding a severely crumpled fender didn't surprise him—his sporty auto could never be a match to the red touring car he'd hit from behind.

He hurried forward just as a tiny woman—she couldn't be over five feet tall—put a foot out on the running board of her auto. Dressed in a fashionable brown-and-cream suit, she reached up to straighten a broad hat of the same colors, tied down with one of those mesh automobile veils.

She stepped to the ground and seemed to be trying to catch her breath when he reached her. Several reddish curls peeked out from under the veil as she looked up at him. She seemed a bit dazed, and he wondered if she was in pain. Little as she was, she probably hurt more than he did. She pushed away one of the curls with trembling fingers.

"Are you all right, miss?"

Her eyes were the deepest green he'd ever seen, and they flashed accusingly as she looked from her auto to his. She took a deep breath and nodded.

"I believe I am." But her voice sounded a little shaky as she continued, "You shouldn't have been following me so closely."

"You should never brake so suddenly. What did you stop for, anyway?"

"A fox ran in front of me."

"Don't you know you should never stop for an animal in the road?" Luke blew out a deep breath as she turned to inspect the back of her touring car.

"What should I have done? The fox wouldn't move. Should I have run right over it?"

"It would have moved." Luke looked at her automobile. The bumper sported a slight dent, but it could be easily repaired. His gaze moved to his own auto. Too bad he couldn't say the same for it. Oh, it could be fixed, but as steam began drifting up from the radiator, he feared it would take more work and money and—

"Papa was right," the young woman said.

"Right about what?"

"He said this touring auto would withstand an accident much better than the sporty roadster I'd wished for." She did have the grace to at least wince as she looked at his roadster.

"Yes, well, it does appear he told the truth." He looked down at her—she barely reached his shoulder—before holding out his hand. "I'm sorry, I've neglected my manners. My name is Luke Johnson, and I'm just moving to Guthrie. I'm going to be living at a boardinghouse there." He looked back at his auto to find the drifting steam turning to bellows. He wasn't going to try to drive it anywhere. "Do you think I might get a ride into town with you so I can send a mechanic out to get mine? Of course, I'll pay for the damage done to your vehicle, too."

She ignored his hand but hesitated only a moment before giving a brief nod. "Yes, I'll give you a ride. I can't leave you to walk—it's at least ten more miles to town. My father will be pleased you are willing to pay for the damage. I am sorry you were following so closely you couldn't stop."

Luke couldn't help but admire her pluck, even though he considered the accident totally her fault. But the fact he'd run into the back of her wouldn't get him very far in convincing anyone else of that fact.

She gave a quick look at the inside of his vehicle. "Do you want to bring your luggage with us? I have plenty of room, and you wouldn't want to take a chance of your things being taken."

"Thank you. That's a good idea." Luke grabbed two cases out of his small roadster and followed her back to her auto. He slung his baggage inside before going to the front of the car. "I'll crank the engine for you."

The young woman nodded, and in only a few moments they were back on the road. Luke hadn't missed the fact she'd never told him her name, but at this point he didn't feel comfortable asking her what it was. And he couldn't help but steal a glance at her every now and then. She was quite lovely. Her green eyes complimented the color of her hair, and her skin was smooth and clear with a hint of freckles across her nose. She turned to him, and he smiled as she caught him looking at her. A pink flush colored her cheeks as she turned her attention back to the road.

"You said you are staying at a boardinghouse. Which one is it?"

"It's Rose's Boardinghouse over on the corner of Noble and Second Street."

She nodded. "I know right where it is."

"I've heard it's the best in town."

She flashed him a smile. "It is. You'll be made to feel right at home there."

Luke wanted to ask where she lived, but she turned her attention back to her driving, and he turned his to the scenery. He liked the area around Guthrie—liked the town itself, even though he considered home to be in Oklahoma City, and he'd be going back as often as possible. But his boss, Leslie Niblack at the *Daily Leader* wanted him here in the capital at least until after the special election. The pressure to get a news story before Frank Greer at the *State Capitol* seemed to have reached a new high. Each editor had one mission, Niblack to help the governor in his efforts to move the capital to the city, and Greer to keep it right where it was. It promised to be an interesting few months.

Luke glanced over at Miss Whoever-she-was and caught her looking at him. Somehow the thought that he might run into her in Guthrie made staying there quite appealing. He wouldn't mind that prospect at all.

❧

Charity wondered what Luke Johnson would think when he found out he would be living in her family's boardinghouse. And that she lived there, too. She felt a twinge of guilt because she hadn't been completely open with Mr. Johnson—she hadn't even told him her name. But he'd find out before the day ended. She couldn't help but steal a glance at him. He was quite nice looking, tall and broad shouldered, with dark hair and sky-blue eyes. . .and a most engaging dimple when he smiled. He appeared quite comfortable with himself—maybe a bit too much so.

Well aware he believed the accident was her fault, Charity

was just as convinced it was his. Maybe that was why she hadn't been as open as she otherwise would have been. Still, she felt a bit sorry his little roadster received so much damage. "Do you want me to take you to the boardinghouse or to a mechanic first?"

"I believe the boardinghouse might be best. Maybe the proprietor can recommend a mechanic, and I can take my bags to my room."

"Yes, that probably would be best. I'm sure they'll be glad to recommend someone." Instead of popping in and telling Hope and Grammy Rose hello as she usually did, she'd go right to work instead. Mr. Johnson could find out she lived there at supper tonight.

While Hope actually ran the boardinghouse, Grammy Rose served as hostess at meals and helped to plan the menus and fussed over them all. She'd be turning seventy soon, and everyone wanted to make things as easy on her as they could—without taking away what mattered most to her. She'd probably fight tooth and nail if they tried.

As they crossed the city limits, Charity felt a sense of homecoming. She liked Oklahoma City a lot, but she felt most comfortable here in Guthrie. She didn't go down a street or into a store without running into someone she'd known most of her life. Today was no exception, as one of her best friends spotted her and waved, taking a long look once she realized a man was riding in her automobile. Charity had no doubt Lizzy Barns would be telephoning her before the day was over to find out just who she'd brought into town.

She pulled her automobile up outside the boardinghouse

and looked at Mr. Johnson. "Here you are."

"Thank you." He got out of the auto and pulled his baggage out from the back. "How do I get in touch with you to see about getting your dent fixed?"

Charity still didn't tell him he'd see her at dinner and only nodded to the building on the next lot. "Right over there. I work for Logan Building and Design Company."

"The name sounds familiar. Isn't there an office in Oklahoma City?"

"There is." He seemed to be waiting for her to say more, but she didn't elaborate.

He gave a small shrug as if he knew she held something back. "All right then. I'll contact you as soon as I get something set up."

"Thank you. I'm not worried about it." She didn't wait for an answer but drove off with a wave. Another moment and she would have told him she'd see him soon.

She parked her car under the big tree shared by both lots and hurried into the office, hoping no one at the boardinghouse had spotted her. Her cousin Matt looked up from his desk as she entered the office. Sixteen years older than she, he'd taken on the roll of big brother to her, and she loved him as one.

"About time you got to work. Who do you think you are—the daughter of the company owner?" he teased.

"I just might be." Charity grinned as she untied her veil and took off her hat, hanging it on the hat rack just inside the door. "I would have been here earlier if I hadn't been in an accident though."

Matt jumped up and came around his desk. "What

happened? Obviously you are all right, but what—"

"I'm fine, but my auto has a dent." She hung her bag beside the hat and went to her desk, which butted up to Matt's.

"How did it happen?"

Charity sank into her chair with a sigh. She felt she'd be answering that question a lot in the next few days. "I stopped to keep from hitting the fox that jumped up on the road and sat staring at me and—"

Matt's eyebrows tried to meet in the center of his forehead as he frowned and groaned at the same time. "Oh Charity, it would have moved."

Did all men think the same way? "How do you know? It wasn't moving when I stopped the auto."

Matt heaved a sigh. "How much damage did it do?"

"The fox didn't do any damage, Matt. The man who ran into the back of me caused the dent."

"The man who ran into the back of you?"

"Yes. But don't worry. He's staying over at the boarding-house, and he said he'd pay for the damage done to my auto. You should see his snappy little roadster. It's nifty, but no match for mine."

"You seem quite happy about that." Her cousin raised an eyebrow in her direction.

Charity wasn't exactly happy, but she was certainly glad her auto wouldn't need as much work as Mr. Johnson's did. She dreaded calling her father and telling him about it as it was. "Well, it was his fault. He followed much too close."

"I'll go take a look at your auto. You sure you are all right?"

"My chest is a little sore and my neck is kind of stiff, but I'll be fine."

He nodded and headed out the door. "I'll give the name of our mechanic to"—he turned back to Charity—"what is his name?"

"It's Luke Johnson. But don't do that, Matt. He doesn't know my name yet, nor does he know we are related or that I live at the boardinghouse."

Matt turned and put both hands on his hips. "You didn't even tell him your name?"

Charity sighed once more. She supposed she'd been rude, but she'd wanted to surprise Mr. Johnson at dinner that night. Why she wasn't sure, but it'd seemed a good idea at the time. "I didn't like his attitude. He seemed to blame *me* for the accident and it was *not* my fault. Besides, I did tell him I work here. I'm sure he'll let me know when he has something set up. He knows I know where to find him if he doesn't. And I'll see him this evening. So please—"

Matt shook his head and chuckled. "I don't know what kind of game you are playing, Charity, but I'll go along with you for now. Still, I'm going to take a look at your dent." He returned before she could do more than send up a quick prayer that he and Mr. Johnson wouldn't run into each other.

"It's not near as bad as I thought it would be. Won't take much to fix your auto's dent. I didn't notice a new auto parked at the boardinghouse, however. He must have already left in it."

Charity shook her head. "His roadster is still out on the highway. Steam billowed out of it when we left it there. He said he'd have a mechanic go bring it in. And he's going to ask Hope or someone at the boardinghouse who to telephone."

"All right." Matt took his seat across from her. "Everyone there knows we use Jed Baxter."

"So now will you relax so I can get to work?" Charity grinned at him. "We've wasted at least half an hour already."

"Not counting how late you were to begin with."

"I'm not counting—are you?"

Matt threw back his head and laughed. "Oh cousin, mine. You are going to be a handful for some man one of these days."

"Not anytime soon, I assure you. I like my life just as it is."

two

Luke liked the room he'd been shown to very much. It was a corner room, warm and cozy, with lots of sunlight and nice bedding. In front of one window sat a comfortable chair and table where he could read the paper or his Bible. Under another window stood a desk where he could put his typewriter and work on his articles. He turned to Hope Caldwell, the manager. "This is nice, Mrs. Caldwell. I think I'll be real comfortable here."

The dark-haired woman who looked to be somewhere in her thirties smiled at him. "Good. There are two women teachers, a single gentleman, and my cousin up here, so it should be fairly quiet for you. Over the years, we added a single-story wing off the back for family—my husband and me and our two children, plus our grandmother Rose live there. So we do have an almost full house. I like to keep one or two rooms vacant for company, just in case my parents or my aunt and uncle come for a day or two. It's very much a family home, and we want you to feel comfortable here."

"I'm sure I will. I—is there a telephone I could use? And could you suggest a mechanic? I need to have my auto picked up and brought into town."

"Oh, of course. Did you have an accident? You didn't have to walk in, did you?"

"I did have an accident, but I got a ride into town."

"That's good. The telephone is in the alcove just under the stairs, and Jed Baxter is the mechanic my family uses. I'm sure he'll be glad to help you. Just ask the operator to connect you to Baxter Motors."

"Thank you."

"You're quite welcome. Oh, and dinner is at six thirty. We ring a bell, but most of the boarders gather in the parlor before then. You are more than welcome to join them, and I'll introduce you at dinner."

"Thank you. I've heard wonderful things about this boardinghouse, and I'm glad you have an opening." Luke felt at home from the moment he entered the foyer of this well-cared-for home. He'd like to take time to fully settle in, but he needed to get in touch with the mechanic and get to work.

He followed Mrs. Caldwell downstairs, and she showed him to the telephone. He quickly contacted the mechanic, who told him he'd send someone to pick his roadster up right away. After making arrangements to stop by that afternoon and find out what needed to be done, he headed to work.

Luke hoped to get back to the boardinghouse before Miss Whatever-her-name-was left work for the day. He wanted to assure her he'd be getting her fender repaired as soon as he could. He'd ask Mr. Baxter to come by and give him an estimate on how much it would cost and how long it would take to fix her auto.

He looked forward to seeing her again—even though he still blamed her for the accident. Surely she knew better than to stop so suddenly on a highway. Of course, there were more horses on the road than autos. It wasn't as if they were in downtown Oklahoma City. She probably hadn't even realized he was behind her.

What was he doing making excuses for her? Just because she was one of the prettiest women he'd ever seen and his chest tightened in a funny way when he'd first looked into those flashing green eyes didn't mean he should go all soft, now did it? She seemed a bit self-absorbed and spoiled, after all.

He needed to put her out of his mind, at least until after work. Mr. Niblack didn't take kindly to his reporters not getting their jobs done. And he seemed particularly intense ever since news came down about the governor holding an election to try to get the capital moved out of Guthrie. He was firmly on the side of moving it to Oklahoma City. Of course the fact that he'd married the governor's daughter the year before probably had as much to do with his stance as politics did.

Niblack and Greer had been rivals in coverage for a long time. Frank Greer began covering politics in the state back during the land run, and he'd be doing all he could to keep the capital right where it'd always been. Only Oklahoma City had about six times the population of Guthrie, and Luke couldn't see how anything could keep the city from becoming the new capital. Neither could his boss. But on the off chance it might happen, Leslie Niblack wanted all of his reporters out covering the citizens' views on the possible move.

After checking in at the office, Luke headed down to the Capitol Café, where he knew several of the state legislators gathered off and on all day. He'd picked up a lot of information for his articles just by joining them for coffee now and again. He'd found most politicians loved talking about their views on just about anything and everything.

Sometimes the conversations got heated even between those in the same party. And most were quite happy to get their names in the paper as often as they could. But today he wondered if they were all in hiding after the governor's announcement about the special election.

Those who were at the coffee shop were fighting mad, and he acquired plenty of quotes for an article from those determined to keep the capital in Guthrie. Maybe tomorrow he'd be able to get the other side. Although Niblack was very much in the governor's corner, he did encourage his reporters to cover both sides. But the paper leaned toward moving the capital, no doubt about it.

Luke's father was also very much in favor of the capital being moved to the city, thinking it would mean much more work for his already successful law firm, and Luke could see his point. Besides, it seemed only fitting that the largest city in the state should be the capital. But in interviewing people, Luke learned not to voice his opinions. He left that for others to do.

As he left the coffee shop, Luke's thoughts once more turned to the lovely young woman he'd run into earlier. The next few months promised to be interesting, to say the least. Not only professionally—but personally. If he could run into Miss—he must find out her name—occasionally, his time here would be even more interesting. He pulled out his pocket watch and sped up his pace back to the office. He needed to put in a full day's work in a shortened day, but he remained determined to find out the name of the pretty redhead before the day ended.

⮜

When the office's familiar ring came through midafternoon, Matt picked up the telephone receiver and looked over at Charity. "Uncle Gabe. . . Uh, yes, yes she got here safely. Of course." Matt motioned her to the telephone and raised an eyebrow in her direction.

Charity looked up from the house plan she was working on and clapped a hand over her mouth as she suddenly remembered she hadn't telephoned her father to let him know she'd arrived safe and sound. Her stomach took a dive as she took hold of the receiver. Blowing out a breath, she sent up a prayer on how to calm him and then tell him about the accident. "Papa! I'm sorry I didn't telephone. I—"

"Charity, you know that is one of the conditions we agreed on if you were to have your own auto and be able to drive yourself back and forth. You *must* let us know you get there safely."

"Yes, sir, I do know, and I truly am sorry, Papa." She meant it. She loved her parents and never wanted to disappoint them. She hated that he'd been worried about her. "Forgive me?"

"Of course I do. But I worry about you. You know that."

"I'm sorry." She wasn't sure what else to say, and she didn't know if anything would help once he found out about the accident.

"Just see it doesn't happen again, young lady."

"I'll try." She figured she might as well get it over with. "Papa, there's something I—"

"I've got to go, dear. A client just walked in the door.

Mama and I will talk to you soon. We love you."

"I love you, too, Papa." She heard the click of the line being disconnected and turned to Matt.

Matt's eyes were filled with sympathy. "I'm sorry. I should have reminded you. We got caught up in talking about your accident—you didn't tell him about it either."

"I tried to, but someone came in, and he had to get off the telephone quickly. I didn't have a chance to tell him about it. Now I get to stew over what he'll say until this evening. I'll telephone him and Mama after dinner." She took a deep breath and let it out. "I hope he doesn't take the auto away from me."

"He's not likely to, Charity." Matt leaned back in his chair and rocked it back and forth. "But he might make you take the train back and forth from here to Oklahoma City for a while."

Charity bit her bottom lip and twirled an errant curl. "Most likely he will. Hopefully I'll still be able to drive around here."

Matt rolled his chair closer to his desk. "You do know how spoiled you are, don't you?" Elbow on his desk, he propped his chin up and grinned at her.

"I do." She shrugged and smiled back. "I can't help it that I'm an only child, you know."

"I suppose not." Matt turned his attention back to the estimate he'd been working on. "Want me to tell Uncle Gabe there really isn't much damage to your auto?"

"I'll let you know after I speak to him this evening." She glanced at the clock on the wall and reluctantly rolled up the house plans she loved working on before getting back to the real job her father paid her to do. She pulled out the company ledger and got down to work. Matt had stuffed several receipts inside, and she began to enter them. The day seemed much longer than most, probably because of the accident, and she found herself looking out the window more often than usual. She found it hard to concentrate as her thoughts flitted from the accident to what her father would say about it to what Mr. Johnson's reaction would be when he saw her at dinner. She half expected him to show up at the office before she and Matt called it a day.

After her third mathematical mistake, Matt intervened. "The accident must have rattled your brain a bit, Charity. Why don't you take off early today?"

She needed no convincing. "Thank you, Matt! I'll make up for it tomorrow, I promise." She tidied her desk and hugged his neck before heading across the lawn to the boardinghouse.

Charity let herself in the back door, calling, "Yoo-hoo, Hope, what's for dinner? It smells delicious, whatever it is."

Her cousin peeked around the corner. "We have a new boarder tonight. I'm welcoming him with roast chicken and dressing and apple pies for dessert."

"I can't wait. I'll make me a cup of tea and then go up and freshen up and come back down to help."

"The kettle is already on. I'll make you a cup. And there's no need to hurry back down. It's all pretty much taking care of itself." Hope pulled the pan of chickens out of the oven and basted them. "Besides, you know I expect Ellie to help."

"She's growing up so fast, Hope. I can't believe she's nearly fifteen now."

"I can't believe it either. My baby is about the same age I was when you were born." She slid the pan back in the oven and began to make them tea.

"Now you're making me feel old," Charity said.

"Hush now. How do you think it makes me feel? You're just nineteen."

"An old maid by some standards."

"You are nowhere near an old maid. But you are a bit picky."

Charity took the cup of tea her cousin handed her and sat down at the kitchen table. "I can't help it if no one measures up to Papa or Uncle Gabe—or even Matt and your Thomas. Most of the young men who've asked to court me are not men at all, but boys who haven't grown up enough to even think about settling down."

"Someone will come along and sweep you off your feet." Hope joined Charity at the table. "The new boarder is very nice looking."

"I know." Charity took a sip of her tea.

"How do you know?"

"I gave him a ride into town."

"You did? He didn't mention—"

"Mr. Johnson doesn't know who I am. And he doesn't know I live here."

"You didn't tell him your name or where you live? Why not, Charity?"

"Well, I guess I felt a bit rebellious. He made me mad, implying I caused the accident. He seems a bit overconfident, and I don't much like his attitude. I just wanted to see his expression when he sees me at the dinner table tonight."

"You were in an accident? Did you have something to do with his auto being disabled?"

"*He* had something to do with the dent in my fender." Charity went on to explain what happened to Hope. "I just couldn't run over the fox, Hope."

"I understand. I wouldn't have been able to either."

"I'm glad someone understands. Seems Matt thought it might be my fault, too."

"Well, I'm just glad no one got hurt. And now I'm very anxious about how Mr. Johnson will react to seeing you here, too."

"He's not home yet, is he?"

"Not that I know of." Hope took a sip of her tea. "I haven't heard anyone come in the front door yet. I showed him to his room, told him what time we have dinner, and then we came back down. He asked to use the telephone so he could put a call in to our mechanic, and then I assume he left for work."

Thankful Matt let her go early, Charity hoped she'd have time to freshen up and get ready for dinner without running into Luke Johnson. "I'll go up the back way and pray I don't run into him." She finished her tea and got up to wash her cup. "Can't wait to see his face when he finds out I live here."

"What are we going to do with you, Charity?"

Rose Edwards came into the room just then and saved Charity from having to answer. "Why, Charity, I thought I heard your voice. It's good to have you home, child."

Rose made the land run in '89, the same time her mother and father had, but she'd lost her husband shortly after. She'd come to work at the boardinghouse soon after it opened, and she'd sold her land to Hope's father, Ben Thompson. She was the only grandmother figure Charity, Hope, and Matt had ever known, and they all loved her dearly.

"It's good to be here, Grammy." Charity kissed her delicate cheek. "Have you been behaving yourself?"

Rose chuckled. "You're a fine one to ask that, Charity. We're two of a kind, aren't we?"

"Oh, you don't know how right you are, Grammy," Hope said. "Come have some tea with me, and I'll tell you what she's up to now."

❧

Charity couldn't remember ever feeling quite so flustered as she did while she got ready for dinner. What would Mr. Johnson think when he saw her at the dinner table? Would he be angry that she hadn't told him she lived here, too? That wasn't her intention at all. And it really didn't matter, did it? She didn't know why she wanted to be so mysterious about everything. She'd never reacted to any other man quite the way she did to him. He just. . .irritated and intrigued her all at the same time.

She took care with her hair, taking it down and putting it up over a mesh roll so her pompadour looked like a cloud around her face. She dressed in one of her favorite dresses—a green-and-pink lawn. Finally satisfied with the way she looked, Charity peeked out the door to make sure no one was in the upper hallway and breathed a sigh of relief to find it empty.

She hurried to the back staircase leading to the kitchen. Once she reached the hallway leading to the family living quarters and kitchen, she felt confident she wouldn't run into Mr. Johnson until they met in the dining room. She rarely used the back staircase that'd been added when the need to expand the boardinghouse arose, but she was glad to be able to use it this evening.

"Charity, what are you sneaking down the back stairs for?" Hope's ten-year-old son, Seth, asked. He came out of the family quarters just as she reached the bottom stair.

"I'm not sneaking, Seth." Not really. It was the family staircase, after all.

"Oh." He looked up the staircase. "I'm not allowed upstairs unless Mama sends me for something. She said maybe one day I can have a room up there."

Charity suppressed the urge to chuckle. "Well, I'd think about it if I were you. You are much closer to the kitchen down here."

He seemed to ponder her words a moment. "True. I'll think on it. I'm glad you're home."

Charity ruffled his hair. "I'm glad to be here."

Hope rang the dinner bell just as they reached the kitchen, and only then did Charity realize how silly she'd been not to tell Mr. Johnson her name. Why, she wasn't going to appear any more mature than those boys who asked to court her.

"Bring the bread basket won't you, Charity?" Hope asked as she picked up the platter of roast chicken. "Ellie and Seth took the side dishes in."

Charity took the napkin-lined basket full of homemade biscuits and followed her cousin into the next room. Thankfully, Luke Johnson stood with his back to her, but her relief lasted only a moment—just until she realized Hope had seated him right next to her. She glared at her cousin, who flashed her a grin. Charity sighed and put the rolls on the table as cousin-in-law Thomas seated Hope.

Before she could pull out her own chair, Mr. Johnson did it for her. "Why good evening, Miss. . . ?" He smiled and raised an eyebrow.

The time for pretense was over. She smiled at him. "Charity Logan, Mr. Johnson. Please forgive my rudeness this morning. I should have told you my name then."

She took the seat, and he quickly slid it forward and whispered in her ear, "I think you were trying to surprise me this evening, weren't you? If so, you pulled it off very well. It's nice to finally have a name to put to your lovely face, Miss Logan."

Charity felt a wash of color rush to her face. Why, did the impudent man think she might be trying to. . .to flirt with him? Worse yet—her heart began to thud—could he be right?

three

Luke took his own seat next to Miss Logan with a certain amount of satisfaction. He thought perhaps he'd surprised her almost as much as her presence had him. He hoped so. It would serve her right for deceiving him. The soft color that crept up her neck began to subside when Mrs. Caldwell stood and addressed her boarders.

"Everyone, we have a new boarder with us tonight." She nodded in Luke's direction and smiled at him. "This is Mr. Luke Johnson, and he will be staying with us for a while."

"Mr. Johnson, this is my husband, Thomas," she put a hand on the arm of the man at the end of the table.

The men exchanged nods as Mrs. Caldwell continued, walking behind each person and touching each one on the shoulder as she introduced them. "This is our son, Seth, and daughter, Ellie. My cousin Charity is next to you, Mr. Johnson."

So these people were Miss Charity's family—she wasn't just a boarder like he was. Very interesting. Mrs. Caldwell went around him and touched the shoulder of a lovely older woman with lively black eyes and hair the color of salt and pepper. "This is our grandmother, Rose."

On the other side of the table sat Mrs. Landers, one of the teachers in town, Mr. Benson, an attorney, and Miss Sawyer, who worked at the telephone office. And it turned out the last couple weren't boarders, but were part of the family, too. "This is my brother, Matt, and his wife, Joy, who often eat with us. They have a son, but he's away at college."

"How do you do everyone? I'm pleased to meet you all, and I'm very glad Mrs. Caldwell had a room to let," Luke smiled and tried to look each person he'd been introduced to in the eye.

"You won't regret staying here, Mr. Johnson. Best boardinghouse in town." Mr. Benson looked to be about the same age as Miss Logan's grandmother. His eyes were bright blue, his gray beard and mustache well trimmed. "Best food in town, too. What is it you do?"

"I'm a reporter for the *Daily Leader*, sir. I mostly cover the political goings-on in the state and in particular up here in Guthrie." Charity's quick intake of breath gave him his first indication the *Leader* wasn't her paper of choice.

"Why, that must be very interesting, especially now with all the hoopla over moving the capital," the older man said.

"Yes, sir. It is."

"I usually read the *State Capitol*, but it'll be nice to have someone in the know to tell us what's going on," Mrs. Landers said. "Sometimes I can't make heads or tails out of all the political talk."

"I think the politicians like it that way, Mrs. Landers," Matt Thompson said.

Mr. Caldwell said the blessing and began carving the chicken while everyone exchanged pleasantries. The food tasted delicious, and the company was quite good, even if Miss Logan said little. Luke was quite happy just sitting beside her. But now the name sounded as familiar as her lovely face seemed to be to him, yet he knew they'd never met before.

While he tried to listen and respond to the conversations going on around him, he racked his brain to try and remember if he and Miss Logan had met before. Could that be why she'd wanted to be so secretive about her name? Was she waiting to see if he remembered her?

As the meal progressed, he leaned over and said, "I talked to a mechanic today. He said he would come look at your auto tomorrow and let me know when he could start work on it."

"Why thank you, Mr. Johnson, I do appreciate your checking with him."

Luke decided paying for her small dent was well worth it when she smiled at him—even if her tone seemed a bit stiff.

"What about your roadster? Is it going to take a while to repair it?" she asked.

"At least a week, possibly longer." More like two or three to his way of thinking.

"That's too bad," Miss Logan's green eyes deepened a shade, and she actually sounded sympathetic. But he felt certain she still blamed him for the accident. And now, living in her family's home—with many family members surrounding them—he wasn't about to go back on his promise to have her vehicle fixed. Nor did he intend to argue over whose fault it was.

"I saw Charity's dent," Matt Thompson said. "It shouldn't take a lot to fix it. I take it your auto suffered more damage?"

To his surprise, Luke found he could chuckle. The damage between the two autos was like night and day. It was hard to call his crumpled fender a dent—not to mention the hood or the damage to his radiator. "You could say that."

"It looked really bad when we left it on the road," Miss Logan said.

"What is this? You two were in an automobile accident?" Mr. Benson asked.

"We were." Luke explained how it happened without placing any blame on Miss Logan. "I'm just thankful neither of us was hurt badly, although I think we'll both be a little stiff and sore tomorrow. And of course I'm paying for any damage done."

"Of course." Miss Sawyer said as if there were no question he would.

"I told Charity she should never stop for an animal," Charity's cousin Matt said, making Luke think he might be a man he'd like to get to know.

"And I told you it didn't move. I couldn't just run over it." Charity glared at her cousin.

"What could you not run over?" the other lady boarder—Luke couldn't remember her last name—asked.

"A fox," he informed her and the rest of the table.

Thomas laughed. "Oh Charity, this part of Oklahoma would be better off without so many of those critters."

Next to him, Miss Logan sighed so deeply Luke was sure it must have come from her toes.

"If you'll all excuse me, I must call Papa and recount my adventure *one* more time for him. Then I sincerely hope we can put this subject to rest." She flung her napkin down and left the table.

Luke felt a spark of remorse for mentioning the fox. He

should have let her tell about it. But as the men around the table shook their heads and began to chuckle, he couldn't help but take some satisfaction that at least some in this house seemed to agree with him: she shouldn't have stopped for the fox.

❧

Charity tried to keep from showing how frustrated she felt as she left the table and went to telephone her father. He'd most likely scold her for stopping, too, and she wanted to get it over with. Handsome as Mr. Logan was, at this moment she wished he lived anywhere but at her family's boardinghouse.

She placed the call with the operator and waited until she'd made a connection. Charity couldn't help but smile when she heard her mother's sweet voice. "Hello, this is the Logan residence."

"It's me, Mama. Did I catch you having dinner?"

"No, Charity dear, we're finished. What is it? Is anything wrong? You rarely telephone us until Friday before you start for home. Papa said you were late getting in and forgot to telephone, but—"

"I'm fine, Mama, but I do need to talk to Papa, if I may."

"Why, of course you may, Charity, what's got into you, dear? As if you couldn't. He's standing right here."

Charity heard muffled voices, as if her mother placed her hand over the receiver as she handed it to her father. Her hand began to shake and her knees went all wobbly as she waited for his greeting.

"Charity, dear. What is it? Nothing has happened since I talked to you, has it?"

"No, Papa. But you got off the telephone before I could tell you what made me late getting here, and. . .well. . .I had a small accident on the way here and—"

"What happened? Why didn't Matt tell me? Are you all right?"

"Papa, I'm fine. But. . ." Charity released a deep breath and repeated the events of the morning for what she hoped would be the very last time. She waited in silence for her father's reaction. And she waited. Then she heard him release a deep sigh.

"Oh Charity, I've told you over and over—"

"I know, Papa. And I'm sorry. The good news is I only have a tiny dent in the back fender and the man who hit me from behind has promised to pay for having it fixed."

"Is he all right? What about his vehicle?"

"He is fine. And you were right. The little roadster I wanted would not be a match for my touring car."

"Oh Charity, how bad is it?"

"Well. . .it's much worse than mine. But it's fixable."

"Do we know this person?"

"Well, I do now. His name is Luke Johnson, and he's a reporter, and he's staying right here at the boardinghouse. So there is no way he'll try to get out of paying and—"

"Is he there now?"

"Yes. Well, I assume so. I left the dining room to make this call and—"

"Please get him. I'd like to talk to him."

"Papa—he's a reporter for the *Daily Leader*!" She felt her father might be sympathetic to Luke and hoped that last tidbit would make him see—

"Now, please, Charity."

She knew not to argue with the tone in her father's voice. "Yes, sir. I'll see if he is still there." Charity laid the receiver down and resisted the urge to stomp her foot. Why did she pick now to telephone? She hurried to the dining room and her heart sank. Mr. Johnson still sat at the table, enjoying a second piece of apple pie from the looks of it. "Mr. Johnson, my father would like to talk to you, if you don't mind."

᳕

Luke almost choked on the piece of pie he'd just put in his mouth and nodded. Swallowing it whole, he took a sip of water and washed it all the way down. "Of course."

He was probably in for it now. No telling what she'd said to her father. He stood up and joined Miss Logan at the doorway. Without a word to him, Charity led him to the phone alcove and picked up the receiver.

"Here he is, Papa." She handed Luke the receiver and moved away, but not far enough that she couldn't hear every word he said.

"Hello, Mr. Logan, sir. Your daughter said you wanted to speak to me. First I must tell you how sorry I am about the acci—"

"No need to apologize, young man. I've told Charity over and over again not to stop for some animal running out onto the road. What I want to know is how badly your vehicle is damaged. I'll be glad to pay—"

"Oh no, sir. It's being taken care of now. And I'll have your daughter's auto fixed next week. I should have been watching up ahead of me better." Normally Luke would never have interrupted an older man, but he could see Charity was upset by the expression on her face, and her beautiful green eyes were turning almost blue. Did they do that only when she became upset?

"Well, I'm not sure whose fault it was, but thank you for taking care of my daughter's vehicle, Mr. Johnson."

"You're welcome, sir. Would you like to speak to your daughter, again?"

"Yes, please."

Luke handed the receiver back to Miss Logan. From the flash of her eyes, he felt certain she wouldn't welcome him staying to listen to the rest of their conversation so he took himself back to the dinning room.

Suddenly it came to him where he'd seen her before and why the Logan name seemed so familiar. He was pretty sure Gabe Logan was the name of the architect his parents wanted to design and build the new home they'd been talking about. And he'd seen Charity's photo in the social section of the paper numerous times. Good thing he'd decided to take responsibility for the accident. The last thing his parents would want would be for him to get on the wrong side of her father if they were still thinking about building.

❧

Not wishing to run into Luke Johnson again that night, Charity hid out in the kitchen and helped Hope, Ellie, and Grammy Rose clean up. They hadn't raised the issue at the dinner table—one of the rules from her parents' time of managing the boardinghouse was that politics should never be discussed at the dinner table because one never knew what side a boarder might be on, and it would be rude to insult them—but finding out Luke Johnson worked for the *Daily Leader* told her he wouldn't be sympathetic to her family's desire to keep the capital right there in Guthrie. She couldn't contain her frustration any longer.

"Too bad you didn't know whom Luke worked for before you gave him a room, Hope," Charity said as she took a plate from Ellie and put it in the cupboard.

Hope turned to her with a quizzical frown. "Why Charity, we've never made it a habit to ask one's political persuasion before renting a room. He seems like a nice man, and just because he works for Niblack doesn't mean he thinks the same way about everything."

Charity felt her eyebrows climb, but she held her tongue, knowing what Hope said was true—at least the part about not asking which political party one belonged to. But right now she wished the rule had never been put in place.

"It will be all right. You'll see." Hope gave her a pat on the shoulder. "You're just put out because he caused your accident. But at least he's going to pay for repairs, Charity."

The fact that he'd taken responsibility for the accident seemed to give everyone the opinion he was a good man—when they really knew nothing about him.

"Sure you don't want to come visit for a while, Charity?" Hope asked when Charity put the last plate up and the kitchen looked spotless.

Charity's parents always made it a habit of having family time in the kitchen after dinner and before bedtime. It'd been the only time they could get together to talk about family things and how their day had gone. Hope had started out carrying on the tradition until she and Thomas had children, and now they retired to their parlor for family time and Charity found she missed gathering in the kitchen. Oh, they almost always asked her to join them, and most nights she did. But she'd talked about the accident all she wanted to for tonight, and she didn't want to discuss the new boarder anymore either.

"I think I'll just go to bed, Hope. It's been a long day." A very long one. First the accident, and then trying to work while worrying about telling her father about it, and then finally doing so. She had no energy or desire to talk about anything else that evening.

"I understand. See you in the morning."

" 'Night, dear," Grammy Rose added. "I'm glad you weren't hurt."

"Good night, everyone." Stiffness had settled in her back, and her neck hurt each time she turned it, but she didn't want to say anything about it. She kissed her grandmother on the cheek and headed up the back staircase a little slower than usual.

Her room was on the front, and when her father had added the new wing, he'd taken the opportunity to add a bathroom to her bedroom and the room across from it. He did it so that when she, or he and her mother or Hope's parents, came to stay, they wouldn't have to share with the boarders. Charity had never been happier to have her own bathroom than tonight. She certainly didn't want to run into Luke Johnson again. Not to mention how her aching body longed for her tub.

After a long soak to try and loosen up her back, she felt a little better. Once she got ready for bed, she eased herself down in the chair and leaned her head back, thinking about the conversation with her father. Although he sounded as loving as always over the telephone, she'd felt he might be disappointed in her. Maybe it was his last words to her before the call ended that made her feel that way.

"Feel blessed this young man is more than willing to pay for the damage and is taking the blame for the accident," he'd said.

"But he—"

"Maybe he wasn't watching as closely as he should have, Charity. But he is taking responsibility for it. I'm just thankful you are all right and he is as well. I love you, Charity. I'll explain everything to your mama, and we'll see you this weekend."

"All right, Papa. I love you, too." She'd hung up the receiver, thankful she didn't have to go over the whole story again. But she knew her mother. She'd be telephoning the next morning to check on her—at least Charity hoped she would.

Oh, she knew her father's first concern was for her, but something about the way Luke talked to him made her believe he'd offered to fix Luke's auto, of all things! And the truth was even if the accident was her fault, it was his, too. She shouldn't have stopped so suddenly, but if he'd been driving at a safe distance behind her, they wouldn't have crashed. Still, she couldn't rid herself of a little niggle of guilt for being so quick to blame him. Tears came to her eyes. Deep down, she knew she was at fault, too. She just didn't want to admit it.

Her heart heavy, she pulled her Bible off the side table and flipped it open. Her gaze rested on Proverbs 30, verse 10: "Accuse not a servant unto his master, lest he curse thee, and thou be found guilty."

Well, Luke Johnson wasn't a servant, but she'd accused him. Still he hadn't cursed her. He'd taken the blame and responsibility for the accident instead. And she knew she was as guilty of causing the accident as he was. Worse, she'd accused him and tried to excuse herself.

Charity slipped to her knees and rested her head on her footstool. "Father, forgive me. I am sorry I so quickly placed blame. Please give me the courage to tell Mr. Johnson I'm sorry and take my part of the blame for his vehicle being so crunched up. I will do it as soon as I see him tomorrow. Thank You for keeping either of us from being injured. In Jesus' name, amen."

Feeling better for admitting her mistake, Charity laid out her clothes for the next day. Now that she knew what she must do, she wanted to get it over with. Maybe then she'd quit thinking about Mr. Johnson so much—and then again, maybe not. Something about the man intrigued her. He seemed a little too confident and cocky at times—as when he flirted at the dinner table, seeming to think she might be interested in him. But when he spoke to her father, he'd seemed quite willing to take responsibility for the accident. She wanted to know what kind of man he really was—a first for her. She couldn't remember ever being quite so interested in any other man.

And she wasn't very happy to be so curious now that she knew where he worked. Nevertheless, she couldn't quit thinking of him. She hoped her cousin was right in suggesting he might not have the same political views his boss held. Because there was no doubt the handsome Luke Johnson made her feel all fluttery on the inside. Made her want to get his attention and make him smile at her—maybe even flirt with her again. Her heart sped up at the thought he might. Oh dear, what was she to do?

four

Charity looked at the clock on the wall of the Capitol Café once more. Lizzy had telephoned early that morning to see if they could meet for breakfast before work, and if her friend didn't get here soon, she'd order without her. Or just leave.

While there were several women in the place, it seemed mostly men came in this time of day, and she wasn't quite comfortable sitting at a table alone. There seemed to be more of an even mix of men and women during the afternoon when many ladies took a break for tea.

About the time she'd decided to leave, her friend swept into the café, her hat all awry on top of her windblown blond hair and a gleam in her brown eyes. Charity knew Lizzy well. She wanted to know who the man she'd given a ride to was. Engaged to her high school sweetheart, Edward White, Lizzy wanted Charity to find someone, too, and probably hoped this new man might be the one. Charity knew she'd be quite disappointed to find out she couldn't be more wrong.

"My, it's windy today!" Lizzy dropped into a chair across from Charity, and before either of them uttered another word, a waiter came to take their order. They quickly asked for buttered toast and coffee, but once he left the table, Lizzy lost no time in getting to her purpose for the meeting. "Now tell me about the handsome man I saw riding into town with you yesterday. Have you found someone at last?"

For a moment Charity felt a twinge of something she couldn't put a name to that made her a little sad. Maybe it was regret that her friend wasn't right. Charity quickly pushed the thought away and smiled at her friend. "Oh Lizzy, isn't it enough you've found someone? I'm not looking for love, and no, I haven't found anyone."

"Oh, Charity! How are we going to raise our future children together if you never get married?"

"I didn't say I'd never get married. I'm just not looking—" She broke off her sentence when she realized her friend's attention was on something outside the window they were sitting next to.

"Well, you might not be looking, but it appears he may be."

The door opened, and in walked Luke Johnson. Charity wasn't prepared for the way her heart skittered and flittered in her chest at the very sight of him. The man was just too handsome for his own good. Just then he looked over in their direction and smiled. He sauntered over and stopped in front of their table.

"Good morning, ladies." Luke tipped his derby to them and smiled. "Miss Logan, your cousin told me you'd met a friend, but she didn't say where. I'm glad to run into you. I wonder if the mechanic might come look at your auto sometime this afternoon so we can find out when he can start on your repairs."

"Of course. I'll be at the office or home once I leave here. Anytime this afternoon should be fine."

"I'll let him know. Hopefully we'll have your dent repaired in a day or two."

No way could Charity miss Lizzy's signal—not the way

she kept jerking her head in Luke's direction. "Please forgive my manners. Mr. Johnson, this is my best friend, Lizzy Barns. Lizzy, this is Mr. Luke Johnson. He's a new boarder at Hope's."

"How do you do, Miss Barns?" Luke turned to Lizzy. "I'm pleased to meet any friend of Miss Logan's."

"I'm pleased to make your acquaintance as well, Mr. Johnson. Will you be staying in Guthrie long?"

"Well, yes. I'm from Oklahoma City, but I work for the *Daily Leader* here in Guthrie."

At the mention of his workplace, Charity raised an eyebrow in Lizzy's direction and got a small shrug back.

"I'll go home most weekends, but I'm so glad to have found a boardinghouse that feels so homey." His gaze caught Charity's and he smiled. "Most everyone has made me feel very welcome there."

Most everyone? Was he saying she hadn't made him feel welcome? And why should she? She didn't run the boardinghouse, and she didn't even know the man.

The waiter brought her and Lizzy's food right then, and Luke tipped his hat once more. "I'll let you ladies enjoy your breakfast. It's nice to meet you, Miss Barns, and I'll see you later, Miss Logan." He turned and waved at a group of men across the room, heading off in their direction.

Charity didn't know if she was pleased to have run into him or not. And when he'd turned away, she'd felt almost dismissed. Luke Johnson both irritated and intrigued her and—

"Oh Charity, he is even better looking up close than from across the street. And he lives at the boardinghouse?"

Trying not to show how much the man flustered her, Charity centered her attention on her friend. "He just moved in yesterday, Lizzy."

"Well, how did you come to know him and give him a ride? And what did he mean repair your auto? Did you meet him in the city?"

"I don't really know him." Charity sighed before telling the whole story all over again. She wished she could just place an article in the newspaper to explain it to the whole town, for it felt as if she was going to have to tell everyone what happened before all was said and done. Maybe she should talk to Luke Johnson about doing that very thing. Except he worked for the wrong paper, and there was no way she'd be giving it any of her money!

"Why, Charity, you mean he's going to pay for your damage and his?"

"Yes. And why shouldn't he? He ran into the back of my auto."

"But you stopped so suddenly—I'm sure he wouldn't have careened into you if he could have helped it. Especially as his roadster has the most damage."

"Lizzy, just whose friend are you anyway? Besides, the man works for—"

"Why I'm your friend of course, and you know I am, Charity. Where he works doesn't mean anything. A reporter is supposed to tell both sides. And you don't know yet what side he'll tell. But don't you feel the least bit sorry about his predicament? He'll be without his auto for a while. At least you can still drive yours."

Friends. Why did they have to be so brutally honest?

Charity did feel bad about driving around when his auto was in the shop. Of course he could hire a hack or catch the streetcar, but that would cost money he needed for repairs. Besides, what happened to her resolve and promise to the Lord just the night before to accept part of the blame for the accident? And to let Mr. Johnson know she did? She sighed and glanced over at Luke. "You're right. I can probably pay for my own repairs, and I suppose I shouldn't have stopped so suddenly. The fox would have moved—hopefully. It's just. . ."

What? The man seemed to blame her? How was that any different than her blaming him? At least he'd offered to pay for her dent. And he'd been very nice to her ever since. More than she could say for the way she'd treated him. And why? Not knowing bothered Charity the most.

❧

Luke tried to concentrate on what representative Moyer was saying but it wasn't easy with Miss Logan and her friend sitting across the way.

"It's just not fair to the people of Guthrie to have the capital taken away. Why, what will happen to the town, if it's moved?" the representative asked the men around him.

"It'll dry up and blow away, most likely," a representative from the panhandle said.

"Oh, it won't be that bad," a member of the other party said. "But it's not going to be good."

Spoken like a true politician. Luke listened for any other replies the representatives might make, but none were forthcoming. Obviously they were all of one accord, no matter what political party they represented. Guthrie wouldn't fare well if the capital was moved.

He would have liked a livelier debate, and with none forthcoming, he couldn't keep from stealing one more glance in Miss Logan's direction. She looked quite lovely today, dressed in a yellow-and-white-striped outfit, which drew ones eye to her beautiful head of hair. Her expression became animated as she talked to her friend in earnest about something. She hadn't seemed very happy to see him, and he wished he knew why he seemed to rub her the wrong way.

The men at his table stood up and began to take their leave, and Luke figured it was time to get to the office and see what kind of article he could pull out of the one-sided opinions he'd just heard.

Miss Logan and her friend appeared to be leaving, too, so he hurried to open the door for them. "Good day, ladies. I hope you have a nice one," he said as they passed through.

"Good day to you, too, Mr. Johnson. It's a pleasure to meet you," Miss Barns said. "I hope we meet again. I'll talk to you later, Charity. I'd better get to work before Mr. Taylor docks me for being late." Charity's friend hurried down the street, leaving Luke and Charity standing next to her auto.

Charity said nothing, and Luke didn't know what to say, so he turned to leave. But suddenly he felt her small hand on his arm.

"Mr. Johnson, I. . .I'm sorry I've appeared so rude ever since you ran into me. I must accept part of the blame for our accident. You were right. I shouldn't have stopped so suddenly. And I don't expect you to pay for my dent. I can take care of it. My father pays me a good wage." She smiled up at him. "I suppose I am a bit reluctant to admit when I am wrong. The Lord is working with me on that."

Something about this woman drew him to her in a way no other ever had. Her complete honesty about what she saw as her shortcomings was totally refreshing. He'd never met another woman who'd ever confessed something like that to him. And yet she frustrated him, too. One moment she seemed to dislike him, and the next she seemed quite genial.

Her hand was still on his arm, and Luke covered it with his own as he looked into her eyes. They quickly turned from deep green to the delightful shade of green-blue again. Suddenly Luke knew he wanted to find out what made them change color. And then he wanted to figure out how to make it happen again.

"I have a few things in my life the Lord is working on me with, too. And I thank you for accepting part of the blame. But I won't let you pay for the damage to your auto. I did hit you, after all. What say we just lay the blame on the ornery fox from now on?"

He'd never heard her laugh before, and the light, tinkling sound filled him with happiness and made him want to hear it again.

"I think that's a wonderful idea. Thank you," Charity said. "I'm heading back to the office now. Can I give you a ride to yours?"

Luke wasn't about to turn her offer down. "I'd appreciate it. My boss is going to wonder where I am as it is. I'll crank the engine for you."

Charity got in the auto, and once the engine rumbled to life, Luke jumped in on the passenger side. The newspaper office was only a few blocks away, but Luke was glad of her offer and her company. He quite enjoyed the curious looks from bystanders when she stopped in front of the newspaper office. Luke jumped out of her auto and leaned back in through the open window. "Thank you again, Miss Logan, I appreciate the ride."

"You're quite welcome. You know, since we're living in the same place, maybe we should dispense with the formalities. Please. . .call me Charity."

"I'd be glad to, but only if you'll call me Luke, Charity."

"I think I can manage to call you Luke. See you tonight."

He gave her a little salute. "See you then."

She smiled back and took off. Oh yes, seeing Charity Logan on a daily basis would make his stay in Guthrie quite enjoyable indeed.

৵

Charity drove off with a smile on her face, glad she'd finally apologized for her rudeness. She had to admit he'd been quite chivalrous about it all.

She tried not to let herself dwell on how much she liked the sound of her name from his husky voice. Or what his smile did to her pulse. No, she wasn't going to think about those things. She'd done the right thing for herself, for him, and for her family. She could see no sense in making things difficult for everyone—especially with them all living under the same roof. Luke was a paying boarder after all.

She returned to the office and threw herself into her work, trying not to think of Luke Johnson. Aggravated as she'd been at Lizzy earlier, she couldn't wait until she could show her the plans she'd drawn up for her. Several months earlier, Lizzy's fiancé had come to Charity, asking if she would be willing to design a home for them as a surprise for Lizzy—for when they could afford it. Lizzy had told him how talented she thought Charity was, and although he planned to pay her for the final plan, Charity and her father had decided from the first it would be their wedding present to the couple.

After all the talk about raising their children together, Charity spent the next few hours working on the sitting room adjacent to the largest bedroom. The space could easily be changed into a nursery once they began to have children. She wanted to include a side plan of what it might look like done up as a nursery.

But when the mechanic showed up late in the afternoon, saying Mr. Johnson had sent him, Luke came to mind again all too easily, as if he'd been right there under the surface all the time.

Mr. Baxter looked her automobile over with her and Matt watching. "It's not bad, but taking into account I've got Mr. Johnson's car to repair, and two others I'm already working on, I won't be able to get to it until the weekend. Can you bring it in on Friday?"

"Of course." Charity could take the train home for the weekend. Once she got home and talked to her father, she might be taking it for a while anyway.

"It's going to take a bit longer for Mr. Johnson's vehicle. His is damaged more than I first thought, and I've got to order a few parts. He'll probably be without his roadster for a while."

Charity felt doubly bad about the damage done to Luke's auto. She should have run over that old fox.

"Good thing you've got this touring car," Mr. Baxter said.

"They can withstand a crash much better than most."

"Yes, that's what I've heard."

Luke showed up just as Mr. Baxter was taking his leave, and the two men talked for a bit before the mechanic left. At Matt's wave, Luke sauntered over.

"I'm sorry the repairs on your vehicle are going to take so long," Charity said. "I can drive you to work and pick you up until mine goes into the shop."

"Thank you, Charity, but the walk does me good. Besides, I can always catch a trolley. If we get rain, I might take you up on your offer, but otherwise, I'll be fine."

"You're sure?"

"We could probably loan you one of the company—"

"Oh, no. I wouldn't think of it, Matt."

Charity breathed a sigh of relief. Although she'd be willing to take him to work if he needed her to, his nearness unsettled her, and she found it hard enough trying not to think about him as it was. "What about the weekend? Were you planning on going home?"

"I'd planned on it, but I might stay here. If I go, I can easily take the train." He turned to Charity. "What about you? Mr. Baxter said he wanted your auto brought in on Friday."

"I'd planned on going home, but I'll talk to my parents and see what they say."

"Well, if you decide to go, maybe we can take the same train."

Charity found she actually wasn't opposed to his idea. She hated traveling by train alone. "Maybe we could. I'll let you know what I decide."

"All right."

Matt seemed to be enjoying listening to them a little too much as he looked from one to the other. Charity felt sure the family would know every word they'd said before nightfall. Well, she'd put a stop to him hearing anything more. "I suppose I'd better get back to work before Matt tells my boss I've been loitering."

"It's quitting time. We've both wasted a good hour. If you don't tell your papa, I won't." Matt grinned. "I'll lock up—you go on."

Charity shook her head. She wasn't going to leave with Luke and give Matt more to talk about. "I need to clear my desk and get my hat and bag. See you at supper, Luke."

"See you then." He smiled and turned toward the boardinghouse.

Matt followed her into the office. "So you two are on first-name basis now? How did that come about?"

Charity quickly cleared off her desk, wanting to get away from Matt's questions. Sometimes her family wanted too much information—and Charity didn't always feel like giving it to them. She shrugged and grabbed her hat and bag from the hat rack. "It makes it easier with us living at the boardinghouse, that's all."

"Oh? I—"

"Bye, Matt, see you in the morning." Charity hurried out the door. She hoped he and Joy weren't going to join them for dinner tonight. There were enough prying eyes and ears at the boardinghouse to deal with as it was.

five

Even without a vehicle, the week sped by for Luke. Evenings getting to know everyone at the boardinghouse were the most enjoyable, but the workday continued to be hectic. Mr. Niblack pushed all his reporters to get out of the office and find something—anything—that would convince the citizens of Guthrie that moving the capital to Oklahoma City would be the right thing to do. The stakes were high, and everyone knew it.

When in session, most of the legislators left town on the weekends unless something special was going on in Guthrie they needed to attend.

"Maybe you should go on home over the weekends, Johnson," Luke's boss said on Wednesday. "With all these legislators leaving for the weekend, maybe you can get a feel for what's going on in Oklahoma City in regard to the election."

"What exactly are you wanting me to look into, sir?"

"You live in the old Logan boardinghouse don't you? They still own it, right?"

"I believe some of the family does, but I don't really know." Luke wondered what Mr. Niblack was getting at. What did where Luke lived have to do with what went on in Oklahoma City?

"And his daughter lives there during the week?"

The fact that Niblack knew where Charity lived rankled Luke for some reason. "Yes, but—"

Niblack waved his hand and gave an impatient sigh. "Rumor has it Gabe Logan is trying to drum up a lot of support for the campaign to keep the capital here."

"I don't know him personally, sir."

"But you know his daughter and some of the rest of his family. Surely they mention things...."

"They haven't so far. I've not heard anything about Mr. Logan—"

"Well, keep your ears open, Johnson. You're sure to hear something eventually. And stay close to his daughter. Sooner or later maybe you'll meet Mr. Logan in person and—"

A knock sounded on the door. Mr. Niblack barked, "Enter!"

One of the paper's star reporters stood at the doorway, and Mr. Niblack motioned the other man into the room, ending the conversation. He dismissed Luke with a quick, "Keep those ears open, Johnson."

Luke took his leave feeling more than a little disgruntled. Why shouldn't Charity's father try to gather support for a cause he believed in? He knew two men who ran newspapers for the very same reason—to get people to come around to their way of thinking—and Niblack was one of them. But staying close to Charity didn't present a hardship at all.

Thursday evening at dinner, Luke asked Charity what she planned to do on the weekend.

"I talked to Mama this afternoon, and she reminded me that one of my friends is having a birthday. We've been invited to dinner to celebrate tomorrow evening, and they've got some kind of party planned for Saturday, so I'm going to catch the four o'clock train."

"Would you mind some company? My boss wants me to see what's going on in the city with the special election."

"The election seems to be all anyone wants to talk about these days. I don't even want to think about it. But no, I wouldn't mind having company on the way home."

"Good. Are you taking your auto in to the shop tomorrow?"

"Yes, bright and early. Lizzy and I are going to have breakfast afterward, and she'll drive me back here. She's off tomorrow. But Matt won't mind driving us to the train station if you want to leave from here. Can you be here by 3:30?"

"I can."

&

The next afternoon, Luke hurried to pack his carpetbag with what he needed to take home, and then he knocked on Charity's door to see if he could take her bag downstairs for her.

"Why thank you, Luke, I was just about to take it down. Matt should be driving around to get us any minute now."

She looked quite pleased he'd come to check on her, and he was glad he had. He took the bag on the floor by the door. "I'll take this on down and see you there."

"All right." She held a brown hat topped with green feathers. "I just need to put my hat on, and then I'll be right there."

She looked beautiful, dressed in a green-and-brown traveling outfit, her hair a cloud of fire around her face. He went downstairs looking forward to the trip home and a chance to talk to her without her family listening to every word. Not that he would say anything untoward. She seemed a bit nervous when they all gathered at the table, and he hoped she'd open up so he could get to know her better on the train ride home.

Matt drove up just as he got downstairs, and they loaded the bags into the back of the auto. Charity came out the back door with Hope and Ellie shadowing her. She turned and gave them both a hug before joining him and Matt. He helped her into the front passenger seat, and after cranking the vehicle for Matt, he jumped into the backseat. They all waved to Hope and her daughter and took off.

It didn't take long to get to the train depot, and as they got out of the auto, Luke turned to Charity. "We don't have to stand in line for tickets. I bought them earlier in the day."

"You didn't have to do that, Luke."

"I know, but it's my fault you don't have your auto and—"

"I thought we decided we were both at fault. You're already paying for the repairs. I'll pay for our tickets—"

"You will not." No way would he let her pay for her ticket—much less his.

"Please, Luke. I don't feel right letting you foot the bill for everything. Papa will be quite upset with me if I do."

Matt openly listened to the conversation with a huge grin on his face, and Luke decided he didn't need anything more to take back to Charity's family. "Why don't we talk about it on the train. I'm sure Matt wants to get home to his wife." Luke picked up both their bags and crooked an arm for Charity to take.

She seemed almost as glad as he felt to get away from her cousin. "Thank you for bringing us, Matt. I'll telephone to let someone know when we'll be back."

"Be sure to. You two have a good time." Matt gave them a wave and drove off.

Charity put her hand through the crook of Luke's arm. "Thank you. Sometimes my family is a little too concerned with my business."

"I've noticed."

She smiled up at him, and his chest swelled with pleasure. "They are so obvious. How could one help but notice?"

He chuckled. "Living in the same place, it's pretty hard not to. But you deal with it well."

They reached the conductor, and Luke pulled out the tickets and gave them to him. Then they boarded the train and found an empty seat. Luke stored their baggage under their seats and sat down beside Charity, who had the window seat.

In what seemed only minutes, the train came to life and began to chug away from the station. They were on their way to the city. Together. And they'd both be returning to the same place. Something about that gave Luke great satisfaction.

❧

Sitting so close to Luke made Charity's heart do some funny things. First it felt as if it stopped; then it sped up, to repeat it all again when he smiled or looked her way. She needed to have a talk with herself about her reaction to this man—just as soon as she could put some distance between them.

She saw several admiring glances aimed toward him from some of the other ladies on the train, and she felt a certain sense of pleasure in being the one seated beside him. But when he answered one or two of their smiles, it irritated her much more than it should have, and her good mood suddenly disappeared.

"So, this is a working weekend for you?" She wondered if she sounded as snippy as she felt.

"Part of it is. Hopefully I'll be able to get material for an article or two. My boss won't be thrilled if I don't come back with something. But I'll manage to enjoy spending time with my family and a few friends, too."

Charity wondered if those friends included women, and the realization that they must bothered her a great deal. She refused to think there might be a special woman in Luke's life, yet she really didn't know him anywhere near well enough that it should matter to her. But as she caught one more woman staring at Luke, she knew it did matter, whether she wanted it to or not.

"You have a party to go to tonight? I wonder if we know any of the same people?" Luke asked, seeming not to notice the looks coming his way.

"My friend's name is Cassandra Billings. Do you know her?"

"The name sounds familiar, but I don't think I know her. I do know a William Billings."

"He's her big brother."

Luke chuckled. "Probably why her name sounds familiar. She must be several years younger than him, though."

"She's my age."

"I don't know your age." His smile washed over her. "How old are you, anyway?"

"Why, Mr. Johnson, don't you know you should never ask a

lady her age?" Charity raised an eyebrow at him.

He leaned nearer, causing her tummy to flutter. "I'm sorry. You are right. My mother has told me that on numerous occasions. But you can't be very old. Not near as old as I am."

Charity fought the urge to ask his age, even biting her lip to keep from doing so.

He must have sensed she wanted to, for he laughed and said. "It's all right, Charity. Far as I know there's no rule against asking a man his age. But just so you don't have to ask, I'm twenty-six."

She'd thought he might be around twenty-one or two. He certainly didn't look much older. But as she thought about it, she realized he'd already acted much more mature than the young men she usually spent time with. Could that be the reason she found herself drawn to him even when she'd thought of him as brash and full of himself?

"Much older than you?" His gaze captured hers as if her answer mattered.

"A few years, is all." Well, maybe more than a few.

"Still not telling?" His smile made her wonder if he might be flirting.

"I might never tell." She felt the corners of her lips turn up. Was she flirting with him? She quickly changed the subject so he wouldn't think she was. . .and so she wouldn't have to answer her own question.

"What about Eleanor White?" Luke asked. "Do you know her? She's the little sister of another of my friends—Ryan."

"No, I don't know her. But I didn't move to the city until I got out of school so most of my good friends are in Guthrie. I met Cassandra and her family through my parents."

"Oh I see. How do you like Oklahoma City?"

"I like it a lot. There is definitely more to do and see there, and the shopping is very good. But I'm glad I get to live both places and haven't had to say good-bye to my friends."

"I can understand that."

"What about you? Do you miss your friends when you are in Guthrie?"

"Not as much as I might have a year or so ago. Many of them are married and beginning to start their families. Their lives are very busy."

"And why haven't you married, Mr. Johnson?" Charity asked and then clapped a hand over her mouth. "I'm sorry. That's about as rude as you asking my age."

"You're forgiven." Luke smiled, but he didn't answer. She couldn't blame him. If he'd asked her the same question, she wouldn't have answered him either. In fact, she would have been quite upset.

The train stopped at Edmond Station and took on more passengers while several others got off the train. When one of the women who boarded the train captured Luke's attention for a moment, as she swished her skirts and gave him a smile, Charity's mood further deteriorated. "What kind of articles is your boss wanting? I'm sure he'd like some stories promoting the election to move the capital."

"What makes you think so?" he asked, a half smile on his lips as he waited for her answer.

Charity laughed. "Luke, I was raised in Guthrie. If there is one thing I know, it's what political view each paper supports. And the one you work for would be that of the governor."

"As a whole, yes, but—"

"Just how do you feel about moving the capital? How are you going to vote on Election Day?"

"Why Charity Logan, I don't believe how I vote is any of your business." Luke chuckled and raised his eyebrow, reminding her she'd admonished him only moments earlier for asking her age.

She caught her breath at her own audacity. He was right. It wasn't any of her business. But it didn't keep the next words from shooting out of her mouth. "I'm sure that means you'll vote for the capital move."

"I was raised in the city, Charity. Maybe I feel as strongly about the capital coming here as you do about keeping it in Guthrie. I'm assuming that's your view?"

"Of course it is. Moving the capital will hurt Guthrie terribly. Can't you see?"

"It might not be so bad."

"Luke, it will be. Businesses that depend on the running of the government from there will fail and close. Hotels, restaurants, and even laundries will shut down. People will move away. It—"

"Oh surely you are exaggerating, Charity."

She could feel her face flush in anger. Why didn't he understand? "It may well be worse, Luke. I don't think I can bear to see my hometown just up and—" She stopped and shook her head. "The city isn't going to hurt if the capital isn't moved there. It will continue to grow and prosper. But Guthrie won't."

Luke only looked at her and shrugged, which made Charity want to stomp her feet. How could he not understand?

The train whistle blew, alerting them they were near the city station. It began to slow as it neared the depot and then ground to a halt in front of the boarding platform.

Relieved to have the trip over with, Charity looked out of the window and began to wave. "Oh, there's Papa and Mama!"

Luke leaned over and looked through the window. "Let me guess. Your mother is the beautiful redhead dressed in blue, and your father is the man standing beside her."

"Right on both accounts," Charity said.

"You look just like her, only younger."

Frustrated as she was with him, he couldn't have said anything that would have touched her more. There was no one she'd rather be like than her mother. But Charity felt certain she fell far short of the woman her mother was. She'd need to grow a lot if she hoped to achieve her goal. And maybe she could start by learning when to keep her mouth closed. This wasn't the time or the place for this conversation. But at least she'd left Luke with no doubt as to how she felt about the stupid election.

They stood and waited until the people across from them stepped into the aisle and moved forward. Luke gathered their bags as Charity waited. But someone behind them came barreling through the aisle and jostled Charity, causing her to lose her balance. Luke carried his bag under his left arm and her bag in the same hand. But he quickly grabbed her arm with his other hand to steady her and guide her out of the train.

"Charity dear, over here!" her mother called.

Charity waved with her free arm. She turned to Luke. "I

can take my bag now. Thank you so—"

Before the handoff could be made, Papa's long stride brought him to them, and he gave her a hug while taking her bag from Luke at the same time. "It's good to have you home, daughter."

Her mother hugged her, too—one would think she'd been gone for weeks instead of days. But she supposed they were thankful she hadn't been hurt in the accident. Luke stood at her side, watching until she realized her parents were waiting to be introduced.

"Oh! I'm sorry. Luke these are my parents, Gabe and Faith Logan. Papa, Mama, this is Mr. Luke Johnson. He—"

"Yes, we know who he is, dear. He's the man who ran into the back of your auto when you stopped suddenly to keep from hitting a fox." Her mother said, smiling at Luke. "Mr. Johnson, I'm glad to meet you."

"Pleased to meet you, ma'am."

Her father held out his hand to Luke. "Thank you for accompanying our daughter home."

"But, Papa, he didn't exactly accompany me. He lives here, too." Charity didn't know why she felt the need to clarify things, but she did.

"Yes, I know, dear. Still"—her father nodded at the bag he'd taken from Luke—"it appears he's been a help to you."

Charity felt the flush of color even before it reached her cheeks. "Yes, he has. Thank you, Luke."

"You're welcome, Charity." He turned to her father. "It's been my pleasure, Mr. Logan. Your daughter was kind enough to accompany me, actually."

Charity felt even worse. The man paid for her train tickets

after all, and she—

"It's an honor to meet you both," Luke said to her parents. "I know from what your daughter has told me you have a party to go to, so I'll be on my way."

"We'll be glad to take you home," her father offered.

Luke looked at Charity. While she did enjoy his company very much, she wasn't at all comfortable with the way her parents were acting. You'd think she was desperately looking for a beau or something. "Papa—"

"Sir, I thank you for your offer, but I have several errands to run before going home." His quick refusal made Charity wonder if she'd hurt his feelings by not insisting they take him home or maybe he really didn't want to ride with them after the way she'd acted. She certainly couldn't blame him if he didn't.

"Of course. I hope you have a nice visit."

"Thank you, sir," Luke replied and tipped his hat. "I'll talk to you later, Charity."

Confused about the way she wanted him to both leave and stay, Charity merely said, "Have a nice weekend."

Luke strode off in the opposite direction.

"He's quite nice looking, Charity," her mother said.

"You think so?"

"I've heard good things about young Johnson," her father said.

"Papa, you haven't been asking about him, have you?"

"I know people who know him, Charity, dear. We know his parents—in fact, they've hired me to build a new home for them. People sometimes come up in conversation. But no, I'm not having him investigated or anything." He grinned at her. "But I do know he's not taken."

"Papa! I am not in the market for a man. They are all. . ." But was Luke like them? Somehow she didn't think so. Charity turned to look for him, but he'd already disappeared from sight.

❧

Luke felt frustrated as he left the train station. It'd been obvious Charity didn't want her parents to give him a ride—didn't even want them talking to him—and he was sure it was because he hadn't given her the answers she wanted. But the truth was he really hadn't thought about what moving the capital to the city would do to Guthrie. He hadn't been able to understand why it mattered so much where the capital was, but after hearing Charity, well, maybe he should try to. He was a reporter after all; he should've already been looking into what effect moving the capital would have on the town.

In any case, he'd gotten the message she'd had all of his company she wanted for one day and made his excuses. Too bad they seemed to be on opposite sides right now. He supposed he couldn't blame her for being out of sorts with him.

After meeting up with several of his reporter friends and trying to find out anything new he could report on going on in the city, Luke headed to his parents' home. He was pleased to find them in and just sitting down to dinner.

His mother jumped up to greet him as if he'd been gone for weeks—when she'd just seen him on Monday morning. She hurried over to him. "Luke, are you sure you're all right after your accident? Your back isn't giving you any problems is it? Should you see a doctor?"

"Mama, I'm fine. No ill effects except for a little stiffness for a few days."

"Then what brings you home? You should have let us know you were coming this weekend—I would have asked Cook to make one of your favorites."

"Mama, I'm sorry I didn't tell you to expect me, but you know anything Cook makes is a favorite of mine—well, except for broccoli and brussels sprouts."

"You're in luck, son," his father said, motioning to Luke's usual seat while his mother went to get another plate for him. "We're not having either tonight. Nor do we ever, if I remember correctly."

"I know. I couldn't resist teasing Mama."

"We assumed you'd be staying in Guthrie until your auto got repaired," his mother said as she set his plate and silverware down for him. "But I'm glad you came—although we have a function to attend tomorrow night." She looked at her husband. "Harold, do you think you could get Luke invited?"

"I'm sure he'd be welcomed."

"Why would I want to go?" He really wasn't in a partying mood and would rather just stay home.

"Well, for one thing, you might get a story out of it."

Luke sat up straight. "Oh? What kind of function is it?"

"The Logans, Gabe Logan, the father of the young lady whose auto you ran into, is hosting a gathering to try and drum up support to help keep the capital in Guthrie. I think there is more to it, though."

"What do you mean?"

"I've heard he's being urged to run for governor next time around. Who knows? He could be trying to judge how much more support he could get."

"Why would you be invited to that? Your politics aren't the same. You want the capital moved here, and from what I've heard, Mr. Logan wants it to stay right where it is. Why would you want to go to his party?"

"All true. But the reason I'm going is because he's agreed to build your mother the home she has her heart set on, and I like the man. It doesn't mean I'd vote for him. But I won't insult him by not attending, son."

"Do you think you can get me invited?" Luke tried not to get his hopes up, but he didn't succeed. This gathering was just the thing Niblack would want him to attend, and it would help him professionally if he got a big story out of it. But even more important to him, he'd get to see Charity Logan again—whether she wanted to see him or not.

six

Ordinarily Charity would have enjoyed the party for her friend Cassandra. But instead, she couldn't wait to get home. She'd been just plain bored all evening. All the young women talked about was the newest fashion styles and who was getting married next. And all of the men seemed years younger than they had just a week or so ago.

When Jim Morrow asked if she'd accompany him to the theater the next night, she quickly told him no.

"Oh please, Charity. The play is getting very good reviews, and it won't be coming to Guthrie. I promise we'll have a good time."

"No thank you, Jim." His persistence exasperated her more than usual. "Papa and Mama are hosting a dinner tomorrow evening, and I'm expected to be there."

At first she'd felt a bit put out when her parents had told her about the dinner party they were having, but now she was relieved to have an excuse to tell Jim no.

Somehow the group she usually spent time with irritated her tonight, and she wasn't even sure why. Maybe it wasn't them, but herself she was disgruntled with. She'd been rude to Luke once again—only not intentionally. She'd just been afraid of what her father might say to him, and she felt nervous with him in her immediate family circle.

Luke confused her in many ways. Half the time she didn't

know if he was flirting with her or teasing in a big-brother way. Maybe because he was older than her, he intimidated her a bit—and yet she hadn't known he was seven years older than her until today.

Yet even after she'd found out Luke's age, she'd felt quite relaxed in his company. She hadn't felt the need to watch every word she said. He seemed comfortable with himself while most of the men she knew still seemed a little awkward and young—at least in comparison to Luke. Was that what unsettled her so? Because he might be more mature and experienced than her, when she felt more grownup than most of her peers?

By the time she and her parents reached home, Charity was exhausted from trying to pretend she was having a good time and trying *not* to think about Luke Johnson.

Most evenings she and her parents gathered in the kitchen to talk over the day, but after a party or special evening out, they gathered in her parent's sitting room just off their bedroom to talk over the evening.

Her mother went on upstairs while Charity went to the kitchen to get the snacks Cook had prepared for them. Her mother must have been listening for her footsteps as she came upstairs, because the door opened before Charity ever reached it. Her mother looked at the tray loaded with cheese and crackers, grapes, and cookies, along with a pot of tea for them and a smaller pot of coffee for her father.

"Cook prepared us a quite a feast, didn't she?" Mama said. "I hope you're hungry. You didn't seem to have much of an appetite tonight."

Charity set the tray on the table beside the sofa in the

sitting room. "You read me too well, Mama. I didn't eat much at the party, but I am hungry now."

Her mother joined her on the small sofa and poured them each a cup of tea while Charity filled her plate with some of everything Cook had prepared. "What is wrong, dear? You've seemed a bit out of sorts ever since you got home."

"I feel out of sorts, and I don't know what's gotten into me lately. I've been looking forward to celebrating with Cassandra, but tonight was so boring. I wish we could've left early."

"There were plenty of young people your age. What did you find boring about the evening?"

"The conversation, the games. . .everything, Mama. They all seem so young."

"Dear, they are the very same people you enjoyed just last weekend and the weekend before. They didn't seem young to you then."

"Oh, most of the men have seemed young for a while now, Mama."

"Hmm." Her mother took a sip of tea. "I see."

"Do you? Because I don't."

"Well, you do live a different life than most of them. Many of them were born to wealth. Your father was just getting his business started when you were born. You've not been raised the way a lot of them have—at least not the friends you've made here. You have more in common with Lizzy and your other friends in Guthrie."

"Perhaps so."

"Probably so. And you do go back and forth to Guthrie. You don't know what everyone is doing here while you are gone and. . .do you think you'd be happier working in your father's office here in the city?"

"Oh no, Mama. Then I'd never see family or friends in Guthrie."

"I know. Do you wish Papa and I had stayed there?"

"Oh Mama, I don't know. I can see you and Papa are happy. And his business here is growing so well. I know this is where you both need to be. But so much has changed in the last few years. Even Guthrie doesn't quite feel the same. It's. . .I don't know for sure where I belong. And now, with all the talk of the capital moving here—oh, I hope it doesn't happen, Mama."

"Neither do we, dear. Your papa is doing all he can to convince anyone he can reach to vote to keep the capital in Guthrie. The dinner tomorrow night is being held for that reason. He's come to know a lot of influential people, and he's trying with all his might to get them to join him in the fight to keep the capital right where it is."

"Do you think it will help?" Charity honestly didn't see how anything could keep it from being moved.

"Well, it isn't going to hurt. I know that much. We'll do what we can to help, and then we'll leave it in the Lord's hands. That's all we can do, dear."

A loud knock sounded on the door, and Charity hurried to answer it. They both knew it was her father—he always gave her and her mother some time to themselves after a party, busying himself in his office and locking up. Then he demanded to join them—as if they wouldn't welcome him. A cool front had moved in and the evening felt on the chilly side, so he lit a fire in the fireplace while her mother poured him a cup of coffee.

For the next hour, they talked about the evening, only not quite so personally as the conversation between Charity and her mother. They also talked about the supper planned for the next night, and her father seemed especially happy she planned on joining them.

"There's something I need to tell you, Charity," her father's tone turned serious. "The get-together we're having tomorrow night is to drum up support to help keep the capital in Guthrie, but if you hear anyone talking about me running for governor in the next election. . .I haven't said yes yet. But a lot of people are urging me to run and the subject might come up. I don't want it to be a surprise to you if it does."

"Governor?" Charity didn't know what to say. She'd never thought about her father running for office of any kind—although she knew he would make a wonderful governor. No one cared more about this state than he did. In fact the state needed someone like him now more than ever. But she wasn't sure how she felt about his announcement. Living in Guthrie, with all the political fighting there, the newspapers duking it out with one vicious headline after another bashing the other side almost every day—she'd come to dislike politics and the reporters who covered them a great deal. Still, she couldn't let him down by her reaction.

She hugged him. "Oh, Papa. I'm not sure what to say."

"Nothing for you to say, dear. Whether or not to run for governor will wait until after we know the outcome of the election."

Her parents had seen many changes in Oklahoma since

they'd come in with the 1889 run. But one change they never wanted to see was the location of the capital. The possibility that Guthrie would not survive had become very real, and now her father was thinking about running for office. Suddenly Charity felt like crying. Her life seemed to be changing in all kinds of ways—whether she liked it or not.

❧

Luke's father easily got his son invited to the Logans' the next night, and Luke was quite pleased to be included. It was a beautiful evening as they drove across town in his father's new Ford. The twilight stretched across the sky, blue-black in the east, changing to deep turquoise, and ending in a glorious sunset of red, orange, and gold in the west. He loved this time of day. By the time they pulled into the Logan driveway, there were already autos and carriages of all kinds parked on the grounds of a home which could only have been built by a master builder.

To say Mr. Logan had talent would be an understatement. Made of brick and local sandstone, his home was full of details that showed the love he'd put into its design. Luke could understand his parents' excitement to have Charity's father designing and building their home.

Not quite as large as the Overholsers' home and the homes of some of the other very rich in the city, the Logan home was every bit as beautiful. Very spacious, the inside was warm and inviting, reminding him of the first time he went to the boardinghouse in Guthrie. He supposed it was Mrs. Logan's touch that made it feel so welcoming.

He looked for Charity but didn't see her anywhere. But he did recognize several state legislators along with some of the more influential men in the city and state. The number of guests made it apparent Mr. Logan was well liked and respected.

Luke moved from one small cluster of people to another and listened to all the talk about how they planned to get the word out to keep the capital in Guthrie—at least for the most part. He felt pretty sure some in attendance would vote for what served their purposes more than on principal.

As he began to hear snippets of conversation, he realized most of those invited also came in on the run. They'd made their way in a new land and prospered by their own hard work. Many moved here from Guthrie, while some still lived there but came in at Mr. Logan's invitation. He became more curious about the man and his past. Where had he come from originally? And what made him decide to make the land run?

As he turned to look for Charity once more, he almost collided with her. "Char—Miss Logan!" He quickly steadied her but kept his hand on her arm. "I wondered if you might have another engagement as I hadn't seen you this evening."

"Why, Lu—" She, too, seemed to give a second thought to calling him by his first name at this kind of gathering. "Mr. Johnson, I didn't know you would be here. You didn't mention—"

"I didn't know I'd be here until this morning," he quickly assured her as she looked at him as if she thought he'd held back something from her. "My parents were invited, and my father asked if I might accompany them."

"Oh. Of course you would be welcomed. How is your weekend going?"

Much better since he'd run into her. "Very well. And you?

Did you enjoy the birthday party last evening?"

"I suppose."

She didn't sound too enthused, and for some reason Luke was pleased. Surely she hadn't spent it with someone special, or her reaction would have been more positive. She looked beautiful dressed in a green gown that looked like silk to him. It made her eyes appear even greener. Her hair was done up in a loose braid wrapped around her head with sweet-smelling flowers tucked into each twist. "You look lovely tonight."

"Thank you." A delicate pink flushed her cheeks, and her eyes seemed to sparkle as she smiled at him. "Would you like some refreshment?"

"I'd love some—if you will join me."

She hesitated for a moment, and Luke thought she might be going to tell him no. But then she looked up at him and smiled. "Of course. I'd be glad to. Mama and Papa have quite a nice buffet laid out in the dining room, where we can help ourselves and eat outside on the terrace. Come with me." She took his arm, and Luke couldn't help but notice the curious glances coming their way as she led him out of the parlor, across the magnificent foyer, and into a huge dining room.

The table was laden with all manner of items, and guests were encouraged to help themselves to deviled eggs; finger sandwiches; salads of all kinds; sliced beef, ham, or turkey; and several different kinds of crusty rolls. On the sideboard were many different desserts, from cakes and pies to cookies and ice cream.

They helped themselves, and then Luke followed Charity outside where round tables were set up for the guests on a large terrace overlooking a huge expanse of lawn and the river in the distance. Her mother waved them over to a table, and Charity hurried across the terrace and quickly set her plate down before hugging the woman beside her mother and the large man who stood and gave her a huge hug.

Charity turned to him. "Mr. Johnson, please meet my uncle and aunt, Ben and Samantha Thompson. These are Hope and Matt's parents, who own the huge orchard and farm on the way to Guthrie. Luke is a reporter who is from here but is now living at the boardinghouse."

He set his plate down and turned to shake Mr. Thompson's hand. "I'm very pleased to meet you."

"We've heard about you, Mr. Johnson. Matt and Hope have both spoken well of you."

"I'm glad to hear it. I love living at the boardinghouse. It feels like home away from home." He pulled Charity's chair out for her and seated her before taking the chair next to hers.

"I love hearing those words, Mr. Johnson," Charity's mother said. "You know it was my boardinghouse and the home where Charity was born."

"I did know. And I can see why it is so hard to get a room there. I feel blessed there was an opening when I needed it." He glanced at Mr. Thompson. "Did you and your wife come in at the same time Mr. and Mrs. Logan did? In the run of '89?"

Charity's uncle nodded toward her mother. "My sister and I were both widowed, and we made the run along with Gabe." He smiled down at his wife. "Sam here, came later."

"And where did you come from, and what did you do before coming here?"

"Kansas," Ben Thompson answered. "I farmed, but not on the scale I do now."

"Mr. Logan, too?"

Suddenly, Charity knocked over her water glass. "Oh, clumsy me! I'm so sorry!"

All three ladies jumped up to try to keep the water from getting on their gowns. Luke hurried to set the glass upright, and a waiter rushed over to quickly change the tablecloth and replace it with a new one. By the time they all took their seats again, several other people had joined them at the table, and the conversation turned to how beautiful the day had been for early April.

❧

The last person Charity had expected—or wanted—to see that evening was Luke Johnson. She'd found it hard enough keeping him out of her thoughts without seeing him in person, and she hadn't been prepared at all for the way the air rushed out of her lungs when she'd first seen him in the parlor. She'd been so taken by surprise at his presence and dismayed by the way her heart sped up at the sight of him she wasn't sure what to do. And she'd wondered how he'd come to be at the party. Did her father invite him, or was he crashing the event in hopes it might garner him a news story? Her suspicions had grown as she'd watched him move from group to group, listening more than talking at each stop. Angered that he might be here only to get a story, she'd been so flustered she'd turned quickly in another direction to try to compose herself before running into him.

She could not deny Luke Johnson was more than a little handsome in evening dress. He appeared taller, his shoulders seemed broader, and his manner more debonair. And after being around all of her male peers the evening before, Charity was forced to admit that Luke seemed decidedly more mature than any other young man she knew.

Charity had moved around the room but managed to hide behind those taller than her as she kept track of where he was. It wasn't hard to do at his height. When she'd felt composed enough to meet up with him, she'd managed to ease behind him and time their meeting for when he turned in her direction. When he did, for a moment she wanted to turn and run. But his smile made her legs go all wobbly, and as she took a step, she must have lost her balance because Luke reached out and steadied her.

Finally, she'd pulled herself together by reminding herself she was the daughter of the host and hostess and had her own role to play. Everything seemed to be going well until he started asking questions about the land run and what her father did in Kansas. Was he just curious, or was he searching for a story of some kind? What was it he was trying to find out? And why did he ask about her father specifically? She'd knocked her water glass over and effectively put an end to his questioning. Not everyone wanted their past brought out, and Charity was very protective of her father's. His past deserved to stay there—and none of it was any of Luke Johnson's business.

Now she felt torn—more so than she'd ever been in her life—wanting to be with Luke, yet needing to put distance between them. But he wanted her to meet his parents, and she couldn't refuse. They went back inside and passed her father looking for her mother.

"We just left her outside with Aunt Samantha and Uncle Ben."

"I'll find them." He looked at Luke. "Glad you could join us tonight, son."

Charity wondered if Luke would ask him for an interview. "Thank you for allowing me to come, sir."

"You're welcome here anytime."

Charity wasn't sure how she felt about the blanket invitation and didn't have time to think about it as Luke led her across the way where he'd spotted his parents talking to another couple.

"I'm sure my mother is telling everyone she knows about the house your father is building for them. I've never seen her so excited about anything, and after seeing your home, I'm thrilled for them."

They crossed the room, dodging first one cluster of people and stopping to exchange pleasantries with another group. But finally they reached his parents, who'd just turned away and noticed their approach. Luke's mother was very nice looking, with dark hair like his, but her eyes were brown. His father's hair was light brown, and it was clear Luke's blue eyes came from him.

"Mama, Papa, this is Miss Charity Logan. She's the young lady whose auto I ran into."

"Oh, Miss Logan, I'm so very glad neither of you was hurt. Luke has told us how much he likes your family's boardinghouse. Isn't it quite amazing he'd be staying there of all places?"

"Yes, ma'am, I suppose it is."

Luke's father chuckled. "He couldn't have reneged on

paying for repairs if he'd wanted to—which of course he didn't. It's nice to meet you, young woman. Your father is building us a new home, you know."

"Yes, Luke told me."

"He is such a talented designer and builder," Mrs. Johnson said. "I feel so fortunate he agreed to work with us. He's included each and every thing I've wanted in the plans, and I can't wait to see it all come together."

Obviously, his parents were excited. Charity's heart swelled with pride at all her father had accomplished in his lifetime. He was living proof that anyone could start over, especially with the Lord in their life.

"Of course I think he is the best designer around. And I know he'll do his best to please you, Mrs. Johnson."

They chatted for a while longer, and Luke's parents seemed very nice. Charity was glad she got to meet them, but was still unsettled by Luke's presence and by her mixed feelings about it all—she felt almost relieved to have the evening come to an end.

Once the last guest was gone, she turned to her parents. "I hope you don't mind if I don't join you this evening. I'm very tired and—"

"Of course not, dear. It has been a whirlwind of a weekend for you—first with the party last night and the supper this evening. You go on up and get a good night's sleep, and we'll see you in the morning."

Her mother agreed with her so quickly and easily, Charity wondered if she knew the last thing she wanted to do was discuss Luke Johnson's unexpected presence in their home that night. She hurried to her room, wishing she could just quit thinking about him.

seven

"It was a good evening overall, don't you think?" Gabe Logan asked his wife. "I think most everyone who came supports keeping the capital right where it is."

"Yes, I do, too, dear."

"I know it's going to take a lot of work, Faith, but if we can get all of our friends and acquaintances to talk to everyone they know and keep it going from one group of family to another. . .who knows? We might stand a chance of keeping it in Guthrie."

"We might. I hope so. But all we can do is try our best, pray—and leave the results to the Lord."

"And we will. We always do."

Faith took the last pin out of her hair, and she brushed it until it gleamed in the lamplight. She was as beautiful to him now as the first day he saw her. He moved to stand behind her and dropped a kiss on the top of her head.

"And what about you running for governor if the capital is moved? What are you hearing about that?"

She wasn't thrilled about the idea of him running for office, he knew. But she'd stand behind whatever decision he eventually made about it because she loved him. Oh, how the Lord had blessed him when He brought Faith into his life. "I think I'd have plenty of backing. I've been assured I'll have support all over the state. Some of these people have been putting my name out there for several years now."

"I know." Faith smiled at him as she moved to take a seat on the couch in their sitting area and patted the space beside her.

Gabe loved this time of day when they relaxed together and talked over anything that came to mind. He joined Faith on the couch as she poured a cup of tea and held it out to him. Gabe shook his head. "No, thank you, dear. I drank what seemed to be a gallon of iced tea this evening." He leaned his head back and then asked the question most on his mind at the moment. "Why do you suppose Charity didn't want to talk over the evening?"

"She's just tired." Faith looked up at him over her teacup. The cup might hide her smile, but he could see it in her eyes. "What other reason could there be?"

Gabe pulled her into the crook of his arm. "You don't think she wanted to avoid talking about young Luke Johnson, do you?"

His wife's laughter never failed to bring joy to his heart. "Now, you know full well it's exactly what she is trying to avoid. Did you see the way they looked at each other?"

Gabe's lips grazed her temple. "Hmm. As if they couldn't tear their gazes away. But I'm not sure either of them realizes how they look at each other—especially Charity. I've the feeling she's trying not to acknowledge it."

"Not to us, not to him, and especially not to herself." Faith put her cup down and laid her head on her husband's shoulder.

"Except she knows there is something different about him." Gabe rubbed his chin on her hair.

"Hmm. And I think he feels the same way."

"Sounds familiar, doesn't it?" Sweet memories of when he and Faith were falling in love surfaced, and his arm around her tightened.

"It does. Are we going to mention it to her?"

"I'm not. At least not yet," Gabe said. "We'll give her some time to tell us."

"How did you get so wise, my love?"

"From living with you all these years, I suppose." He tipped her head up and touched his lips to hers.

"You do know all the right things to say, Gabe Logan. I just pray whoever captures our daughter's heart is someone who'll make her as happy as you've made me."

"I can assure you the feeling is shared, my love."

❧

When Charity entered church the next morning, she spotted a familiar head a few pews over. Luke was sitting with his parents. He glanced her way, and she wasn't sure who was more startled to see the other—her or Luke. Her parents didn't look at all surprised, and neither did his. But why hadn't she noticed Luke before now? If he was a member here, surely they'd been coming to the same church when they were in town. How could they have missed seeing each other before now?

Finally she could stand it no longer. She leaned toward her mother and whispered, "Have the Johnsons been coming to church here?"

"Yes, dear. They've been since before we moved here. But they usually sit upstairs. It's a large congregation, dear. We still don't know everyone."

But the fact that Luke was there gave Charity pause for thought—she'd wondered about his motives the evening before, and it wasn't until just this moment that she realized Luke probably had no motives for showing up at her parents' home except for the fact that his parents wanted him to accompany them, just as her parents had wanted her to be there. Why was she so willing to think the worst of him when he'd given her no real cause to do so?

Her mother nudged her to stand for the closing song, and Charity quickly jumped to her feet. She felt awful—she'd missed the entire sermon with all her woolgathering. *Dear Lord, please forgive me.* Luke seemed to take up more of her thoughts lately, and she determined once more to quit thinking about him.

Much easier said than done when he headed in their direction. Luke smiled as he approached Charity and her parents. "I can't believe we've been coming to the same church all this time and I didn't know it."

"I'm just as surprised. But Mama says your family usually sits upstairs—"

"We do. But when I found out you and your parents attend here, too, I thought I'd sit near enough to talk to you after services and see what time you want to get to the train station for the trip back this afternoon. Have you decided?"

"Oh, Luke, I'm not going to be going back today."

"No?" He looked a little crestfallen, and Charity felt flattered he seemed to care that she wouldn't be joining him for the ride back.

"I'm sorry, son. Her mother and I talked her into staying one more night. I've got to go discuss a few things with Matt tomorrow, and I'll drive her in first thing in the morning. I'd be glad to take you as well, if you'd like to stay over."

For some reason, her father took to Luke, and Charity wasn't sure why. Worse—she didn't know how she felt about it.

"I'd love to, sir. But Mr. Niblack will expect me back in the office first thing in the morning. I hope it will be all right with you if I report on your efforts to keep the capital in Guthrie?"

"Of course. The more we can get the word out about how much each vote means, the better."

"I'd sure like to know more about your plan, and I would have liked to ride with you so I could interview you, but—"

"I'm sure I can make time for you before I leave to come home tomorrow if you'd like?"

"Oh yes, sir. Anytime you say will be fine."

Charity didn't know whether to be relieved or disappointed when Luke turned down the offer of a ride back to Guthrie, but she knew she wasn't the least bit pleased he'd asked her father for an interview—and even less happy when her father agreed to meet with him for coffee the next afternoon. Luke was up to something, she felt sure of it. Her misgivings swiftly flared again.

What was her father thinking, giving him an interview? It might be different if Luke worked for the *State Capitol*, but he didn't. He worked for an editor who wanted the capital moved! And they didn't know Luke well enough to know what he would do with any information her father might give him—surely Papa realized that. What would happen if his past rose up again? His business could be hurt worse than moving the capital could harm Guthrie. And she didn't even want to think what it might do to his chances of running for governor.

She tried not to show her concern as she watched the two men shake hands, but after they'd said their good-byes and walked toward her father's Ford, she mentioned it to her mother.

"Oh, Charity dear, all that was long ago. Your father is much more concerned with getting support to keep the capital in Guthrie than he is anything in his past. And as for his run for office, you know he's not decided for sure yet. So don't you worry—your papa knows what he is doing, dear."

Charity sighed. She prayed her mother was right. Her parents might not be concerned about her father's past being spread all over the newspapers, but what about her? Those who settled Guthrie at the same time her parents did might have forgotten all they knew about it, but others in the state, and especially those near her age, wouldn't know. It would be news to them. And deep down, Charity didn't want them to find out. Didn't want Luke to know. Suddenly she was face-to-face with her own selfishness. What kind of daughter was she, anyway?

❧

Since Charity wouldn't be traveling with him, Luke spent the afternoon at his parents', looking over their house plans—his mother showed him each and every little detail she'd asked for and Mr. Logan had agreed to include—and then he enjoyed Sunday supper with them before taking a later train back to Guthrie.

At the boardinghouse, he'd been welcomed back like one of the family, and he was quite pleased Mrs. Caldwell had saved him a piece of coconut cake. She and her husband kept him company while he ate in the kitchen.

"I met your parents this weekend, Mrs. Caldwell. They're very nice."

She smiled as she refilled his cup of coffee. "Thank you. I certainly think so. But how did you meet them?"

"They were at Mr. and Mrs. Logans'—my parents were invited for a supper, and I tagged along." Luke sniffed the rich aroma of coffee and took a sip from his cup.

"Oh, I'm pleased you got to meet them. And I'm glad they went into the city. Their busy season will be on them before you know it, and they don't have a lot of free time then."

Luke nodded. "You know I've passed his farm many times and admired how well kept and productive it was. It must have taken years of work to get it to the point it is now."

"Oh, it did. Of course, it didn't hurt that he has a natural gift for farming. It's what he always wanted to do, but I don't think even he realized how the Lord would bless him with it."

"He came in on the first day, right?"

"He did. He and Charity's father came in and claimed lots right next to each other. Only Papa always wanted to farm so he put the claim in Aunt Faith's name. And she had a real knack for making people feel at home."

"I could see that this weekend."

"Isn't their home lovely? Uncle Gabe is a wonderful designer and builder, and Aunt Faith has decorated it beautifully."

"Did Mr. Logan and your father know each other before the run, or did they become friends that first day?" Luke never got enough of hearing about how his state was settled.

"Actually, Uncle Gabe helped us get across the river. I still remember it. The river was raging, and most everyone encountered problems crossing. Uncle Gabe rode up on a horse and helped us over." Hope laughed. "From what Aunt Faith has told me, I think he became her hero right then and there. But it took him awhile to convince her of it."

Luke smiled. It'd been obvious to him Charity's parents cared a great deal about each other. . .and their daughter. "They seem quite happy together."

"They are."

"Your parents do, too."

"Yes, they love each other very much. Although Samantha isn't my real mother. She passed away before we came out here. And Papa was so lonely when they met—Matt and I were both thrilled when they fell in love and got married."

"Good marriages seem to run in your family."

She and Thomas clasped each other's hands and smiled at one another. "That's because we all take our vows seriously and look to the Lord to guide us."

Luke was glad his parents did, too. And they'd instilled in him the desire to have the same kind of marriage. Up until very recently, he hadn't met anyone he thought it might be possible with. And even now he wasn't sure. How did one know for certain? And how did one find out if the woman in question could ever feel the same way?

The question still rolled around in his mind on Monday morning. Luke set off for work in a good mood, and he knew it was because he'd be seeing Charity later in the day. He'd never met a woman so full of spunk and yet so seemingly vulnerable. She also seemed a bit spoiled, but not so much that she thought the world owed her. She did work for her father, after all. Many of the young women he'd met seemed interested only in going on endless shopping trips and flitting from one social event to another, looking for an eligible mate.

But Charity Logan didn't seem to be looking for a husband at all from what he could tell. She'd received many admiring glances at her parents' on Saturday evening, but she hadn't noticed. He would have liked to believe it was because she was enthralled with him, but content with who he was, even Luke didn't have that kind of ego. Still, he felt she might be as confused about her feelings as he was about his.

Charity was very different from any other woman he'd met, and there was no denying his interest in her was growing day by day. They might not be meant for each other, but Luke knew he would always regret it if he didn't try to find out whether they were.

eight

Charity enjoyed the extra time with her parents on Sunday, but she couldn't deny she was glad to get home to Guthrie the next day. She tried to tell herself it wasn't because she wanted to see Luke Johnson so much as she wanted to find out what Luke wanted to talk to her father about—if she could. It wasn't as if her papa took her in his confidence about those kinds of things. To him she would always be his little girl—even though he and her mother raised her to be a woman of strong character and to make her own decisions. He certainly wasn't looking to her for advice on how to handle a reporter.

Still, Charity looked forward to seeing the handsome reporter once more. She felt an almost desperate desire to find out what kind of man Luke really was. Her conflicting feelings about him were wearing on her. She wanted to believe she could trust him not to hurt her father or anyone in her family. But it was difficult to do when he worked for a paper that seemed to be against everything her father believed in.

When they got to the office, Papa looked over her plans for Lizzy's house while she waited nervously for his opinion. He went over each room, studying the layout closely.

"You've done a fine job, Charity. It's as good as mine or Matt's first plans. Lizzy and Edward are going to love it."

"Thank you, Papa."

"I mean what I say. You'll be designing right alongside Matt or me one day soon, Charity. I'm real proud of you."

"You've taught me everything I know, Papa."

"Maybe. But you show a special talent on your own," he said, giving her a hug.

Her heart swelled with happiness at his encouraging words.

"I'd best go see how Matt is coming on his plans."

A while later, Charity looked over at Papa and Matt, studying the plans to a new building they were about to start work on downtown. They were in deep conversation, and she admired their ability to concentrate on the job at hand. Would that she could do the same, but her thoughts seemed to flit from one thing to another.

Happy as she was with her father's approval, there were so many uncertainties in her life she couldn't even sort them all out—much less resolve them. Uppermost in her mind was Luke. She didn't want to think the worst of him. She wanted. . . Charity shook her head and pulled her ledger toward her. That was her problem. She wasn't sure exactly what she wanted. All she really knew was her heart longed for something as never before, and it all seemed centered around Luke Johnson.

⋧

Luke half expected to see Charity show up with her father at the Capitol Café that afternoon, and when she didn't, the way his heart plummeted told him he was more disappointed than he had a right to be. Still, he'd see her that evening, and this way he could ask her father whatever came to mind without worrying about how she would react. For some reason he felt she didn't like him interviewing her father, but he didn't know why.

As Mr. Logan approached the table, Luke stood up. The two men shook hands, but before they ever took their seats, several others greeted Gabe Logan as old friends.

Several minutes later, Mr. Logan excused himself. "Look fellows, I've got an appointment with this young man. I'll join you all for a cup of coffee when we get through, if it's all right?"

"Sure, Gabe. You go on with your business. We'll be here when you get through," one of the old-timers said.

Luke breathed a sigh of relief when the men returned to their tables. Mr. Logan motioned to the waitress to bring coffee and then took a seat. Luke took that as his cue to sit back down.

"Well, son, let's get down to business. What is it you want to know about me?" Mr. Logan's smile was contagious, and Luke began to relax.

"Sir, I'd like to know anything you'd like to tell me about how you came to settle in Guthrie and how you've built up your business to the point you are one of the most sought-after builders in the state." He grinned at the older man. "And maybe if you've decided to run for office?"

Mr. Logan threw back his head and laughed. "Hmm. That's a big order. Well, we may not be able to cover it all today, but we can get a start. What do you want to know first?"

"What made you want to make the land run, sir?"

Mr. Logan got a faraway look in his eyes, and for a moment Luke thought he saw a shadow of sadness lurking there. But Mr. Logan gave a little shake to his head and shrugged. "I had nothing to keep me in Kansas. The time seemed right, and I wanted a new start."

"I talked to Hope and her husband last night. They said you and her father came in at the same time?"

"Yes, we did." Mr. Logan took a sip of coffee and went on to describe the run that day and how they'd thought they weren't going to get a lot in town. But then they came across two on what turned out to be the outskirts of town at that time, and they hurried to claim them as their own. "Those are where the boardinghouse and my office stand today. Good lots they turned out to be."

"Yes, sir. What about your business? How long did it take to get up and running?"

"Oh, not long at all. Once people saw Faith's boardinghouse going up, I began to get requests to build homes and other businesses. I've had all the work I could do ever since."

"And now you have two offices in the state?" Luke took notes as fast as he could, not wanting to waste any interview time.

"That's right. I have more people working for me in Oklahoma City just because it's growing faster and there is more business there. The work there got to be enough that I needed to be in the city. Matt is a great architect in his own right, and he has more than enough business to keep this office going."

"And do you think that will still be the case if the capital is moved?"

"I don't know. And it bothers me a great deal. I'm going to

do all I can to persuade people to vote to keep it right where it is. This town means too much to me and my family not to try my best."

Luke nodded. He might feel the same way if he'd settled this town. "Now, what about those rumors you might run for governor one day?"

"I'm thinking on it. Haven't made up my mind yet."

"Would it be too presumptuous of me to ask if you'd let me know when you make your decision?"

The man looked at him, seeming to take his measure before answering. "It might be. But I like your straightforwardness, son. I'll be sure to let you know when I decide what I'm going to do. And next time we talk, I might even tell you all the pros and cons I'll consider when making that decision."

"Thank you, sir. I'd sure appreciate it."

"Anything else I can answer for you, today?" Mr. Logan asked.

"I think you've covered most of it. If there's anything else you think I might want to know, I'd be glad for you to give me a call. I'll meet you anywhere, anytime, sir."

"Sounds good to me." Mr. Logan stood and held out his hand. "I look forward to reading your article, son."

Luke stood and the two men shook hands. "Thank you, sir. I hope to do you justice in it."

"I can't ask for more from you. I'll be leaving as soon as I talk to these gents for a bit. Will you tell my daughter I'll be sure to let her know I got home safe?"

Luke chuckled. "I will be glad to, sir."

He'd gained a new respect for Charity's father as he watched him walk across the room to visit with his friends.

One couldn't help but admire the men who settled this land, who continued to do what they thought best for it and for their families. He'd like to see Mr. Logan run for governor one of these days. His father might not vote for him, but Gabe Logan was a man Luke thought he could vote for.

He gathered up his pad and pencils and headed out the door. He'd go over his notes when he got back to the office and add anything he'd missed writing down. Then he'd start putting the article together this evening after supper. He turned toward the newspaper office, a spring in his step. His interview gave him the makings of a great article, and he looked forward to having dinner with Mr. Logan's daughter. He couldn't ask for a much better day.

***

Charity had been on pins and needles ever since her father kissed her good-bye and left to meet Luke. He'd be leaving for home from the appointment, so she wouldn't be able to judge how the interview went—at least not from his perspective. But maybe she'd be able to tell something from their conversation when he called that night—or maybe she could get an idea from Luke as to how it went for him.

As she finished adding one column of numbers and rechecking her work, she finally realized if Luke somehow disappointed her father in his questioning, she would find out—if not from her father then surely from her mother. She breathed a sigh of relief, and by the time she quit for the day, she looked forward to dinner in anticipation of seeing if she could find out anything from Luke.

Hope had supper well underway by the time Charity freshened up and came back down to the kitchen. It was only a matter of helping to put dishes on the table and having Thomas ring the dinner bell.

All the boarders came in except for Luke, and Charity tried to tamp down the surge of disappointment she felt because he wasn't there. Thomas had said the blessing and begun serving thick slices of the ham Hope had baked when the front door burst open and Luke hurried into the dining room to take his seat beside Charity.

"I'm sorry I'm so late." He turned to her. "After the interview, I went back to the office to start putting my notes together and lost track of time."

He seemed quite pleased, and Charity breathed a sigh of relief that the interview seemed to have gone well. Of course she'd know more once she heard Papa's voice, but for now she'd assume the article would be favorable to her father.

"Don't worry, Luke," Hope said. "I'd have saved you a plate if you didn't make it home for supper."

"Thank you, Hope. I appreciate it, and I didn't for one moment think I'd go to bed hungry tonight, but I sure am glad I get to have dinner with all of you."

"Will Papa be late getting home, do you think?" He never liked to be late if her mother expected him at a certain time.

"I doubt it. He went to talk to some friends when I left the café, but he mentioned he wanted to get home in time for supper."

"Good. Mama doesn't like to eat alone."

"Neither do I," Luke said as took the bowl of creamed potatoes and helped himself before passing it on to Charity.

"So what kind of interview did you have with Uncle Gabe?" Hope asked.

"Oh, about the day he and your father came into town and about how he's working hard to try to keep Guthrie the capital, trying to get friends and family to spread the word along to their friends and family and their neighbors— holding get-togethers to explain why it is so important to him, to them, and to Guthrie."

"Oh I see," Thomas nodded.

"Only problem is Mr. Niblack wants me to expand my article to a series and travel to some other cities in the state to see if anything like that is going on in them, which means I'll be out of town for the next few days."

"Where all is he wanting you to go?" Thomas asked.

"Over to Tulsa and to Stillwater, maybe even to Yukon and Shawnee."

"Then you'll be gone most of this week?" Hope asked.

"Yes. It appears so. Maybe I can talk him into letting me spread it over a few weeks so I'm not gone too many nights at a time. That's what I'm hoping, but I don't know if I'll be successful."

Charity's heart seemed to plunge to her toes. She wasn't at all happy about Luke being gone part of the week—even though she told herself it would make life easier for her if he wasn't there—maybe she could get the way he made her feel into some kind of perspective. But it didn't help much. She had a feeling he'd be on her mind even more in his absence.

As everyone began to enjoy the meal, Luke turned to Charity. "Your father gave me a great interview, Charity. You must be very proud of him."

"Oh I am. I love my parents—my whole family. They've all worked very hard to get to where they are, and they love this state they helped to settle."

"Yes, they do. It's obvious they only want the best for the state. . .and for the town they helped to settle."

He looked totally sincere, and Charity felt a welcome calmness steal over her. Luke wasn't out to harm her or her family. He was only here because he worked in Guthrie. He had no ulterior motive for being at Hope's, for running into the back of her—or for asking her father for an interview. She needed to stop being so suspicious of him and get to know him better instead. Only problem was she couldn't get to know him any better with him out of town.

nine

Luke was happy with how his finished article about Mr. Logan was received by his boss. Mr. Niblack might have wished for a negative article about Mr. Logan, but at the same time, he seemed to admire those who'd settled this town and the state.

"I suppose it won't hurt our readership to have a few positive articles about Mr. Logan. Might gain a few who like him but are open to the capital move."

Luke didn't much like his reasoning, but at least he seemed to be pleased with his writing. Niblack decided to print the Logan interview in installments to give Luke time to get his other articles in. The first one came out in Tuesday afternoon's paper, the second in Wednesday's. On Thursday, the article about an effort by Stillwater's citizens to get on the ballot was snapped up all over the state.

When Luke called in on Thursday evening from Tulsa, he found Mr. Niblack's tone totally different from before the Logan articles. "You've done a good job, Johnson. I think you've hit on an idea we can keep moving up until the election in June. That's the plan, anyway. If you think you can keep up with what is going on with the contacts you've made over the telephone and by visiting one each week or so—with the city more often, of course, since you are from there—I'm giving you free rein to write your articles."

Luke's chest swelled with satisfaction at the acknowl-edgement of the good job he'd done. "Why thank you, sir. I'll make it a point to keep in touch with the contacts I've made and hopefully will continue to make. You might want to know there is a groundswell of anger at Governor Haskell over his trying to push Oklahoma City as the capital. Most want it to stay where it is, but a lot of these towns figure if it's going to be moved, they should have as good a shot at it as Oklahoma City."

"I'll let him know. Actually he's hoping your approach will bring new readers to the *Daily Leader*. Maybe through my editorials, they'll begin to understand what his thinking is and why he called for the election." Just hearing his boss's words made Luke feel disloyal to the Logan family—even though he still wasn't sure how he felt about moving the capital.

"And if you find out there was more to the Logan prison time than we know, I trust you'll follow up on it."

"Prison time? Who?"

"You didn't know Gabe Logan spent time in jail? I thought everyone knew he spent time in prison for shooting a man."

"I'm not from here, remember? What'd the man do?"

"He shot Logan's fiancée back before the '89 run, but it was in all the papers here at one time."

"How did it all come about?"

"Bank robbery. She evidently got caught in the middle of it and died. Logan made it his mission to find him, then shot him."

Luke thought there might be more to the story. "But he got cleared?"

"Yes. After it was proven the other man was the robber and his fiancée's killer. I'm just sayin' if you find out any different let me know." The line went dead, and Luke figured Niblack had said all he wanted to.

Luke replaced the telephone receiver with a heavy heart. He wasn't going to set out to hurt Gabe Logan—from what he'd just been told, it sounded like he'd suffered enough heartache in his lifetime.

❧

Over the next couple of weeks, all the buzz was about Luke's articles about Charity's father and about his efforts and those going on in other towns in Oklahoma to keep the capital right where it was. Luke no longer encountered any problems in acquiring interviews with the legislators.

True to his word, Mr. Niblack gave him complete freedom in what articles to write and what angle to take with them— at least for now. The articles he wrote were being dispatched to the Associated Press, and he'd even received a few job offers because of them. Mr. Niblack raised his pay, and Luke felt his career was taking off.

Life was good, and the best part was getting to know Charity better. His auto was repaired, enabling him to offer Charity a ride into the city on the weekends, and to his astonishment, she usually took him up on his offer.

He knew her father didn't really like her driving by herself, and he used that knowledge to his advantage, but deep down he hoped she enjoyed riding with him. They talked about everything and anything that came to mind, and he felt they were coming to know each other better with each trip.

As the weather warmed, several nights a week someone

suggested going down to the ice-cream parlor, and Luke took to going with them—mostly because Charity went. The first night, he managed to leave the parlor right after Charity did, and to his surprise, she waited to walk back to the boardinghouse with him.

"What else is there to do here of an evening?" he asked.

"This time of year, there's canoeing or fishing along the Cottonwood, picnics and concerts in the park, performances at the Brooks and McKennon Opera Houses. We might not have as much to do as the city does, but we think there's plenty to do. And it's not as spread out as in the city."

She sounded a little defensive, and with all the pros for moving the capital his paper had put out lately, Luke supposed he couldn't blame her. "It is nice most of it is in walking distance from the boardinghouse. I. . .would you like to go canoeing with me one evening?"

For a moment, he thought she might refuse, but then she gave a quick nod. "That could be fun. I haven't been canoeing in a while."

"How about tomorrow evening?" Luke didn't want to give her a chance to change her mind.

"All right. It should be a nice evening for it."

She was right. The next evening was perfect for canoeing. Luke held her hand to help her into the canoe, but the boat bobbled and she lost her footing. Luke's arms quickly went around her to steady her, and he looked down into those eyes he felt he could drown in. He wondered if she could feel his heart hammering at her nearness.

"That was close," she whispered, her lips only a breath away from his.

"It was." If he dipped his head just so—Luke swallowed hard. He could not kiss her—not standing in the middle of a none-too-steady canoe as it was. If she slapped him for his forwardness, they'd land in the creek for sure. He eased Charity down onto the seat and gingerly took the one across from her.

"For a moment I thought we were both going to end up drenched," Charity said with a self-conscious giggle.

"So did I." He chuckled and took up an oar. A slight breeze cooled the air off the water and helped steer the canoe down the creek. The boat slid over the water, and Luke was more than pleased to have Charity all to himself. "Would you like a ride into the city tomorrow?"

"Yes, if you don't mind."

"I wouldn't have asked if I did. Will you be at the Williamsons' tomorrow night?"

"I believe Mama mentioned we were invited. Are you going?"

"I think so." Luke hesitated only a moment before adding, "If you are going to be there."

He couldn't read her reaction as she quickly dipped her oar into the water. "I'll see you there then, I suppose." Only then did she glance back at him with a smile.

His chest tightened, and he wondered how much longer he could put off trying to find out how she felt about him—or telling her how he felt about her. "You'll see me there."

Perhaps he could think of a future with Charity—if she'd ever give him any real encouragement.

❧

For a moment, Charity thought Luke might kiss her, and her

heart seemed to flip and dip into her stomach. But much as she wished he had, she was determined not to let herself fall in love with him. She wasn't sure she'd ever make a good wife for any man. All the submissive stuff in the Bible seemed almost impossible for an independent woman like herself. Yet she wanted the same kind of relationship her parents had, what her aunt and uncle had as well. But her greatest fear was she'd never have it, wouldn't know the right man if he fell at her feet, and couldn't be a good wife if she did. And she couldn't bring herself to talk to her mother about it for fear of disappointing her.

Still, she couldn't help but look forward to seeing Luke the next evening. She'd come to anticipate sitting next to him as they shared meals at the boardinghouse, telling him goodnight at the end of each day. And if he was out on assignment of some kind, she didn't go to sleep until she heard his footsteps on the stairs and down the hall. Only after his door opened and closed could she drift off to sleep. Only to herself did she admit she was beginning to care a great deal for the man.

Although none of his articles came out in favor of the capital move and his articles about her father had been very complimentary, she still wondered if he knew about her father's past and was just waiting to write about it.

She dipped her oar in the water and looked over at him. "Luke. . ."

"Yes? What is it?"

She shook her head. She couldn't bring herself to ask, didn't even know how to go about it. What would she say? Do you know my father spent time in jail? Do you know about my father's past? She couldn't. If he didn't know, then he'd become more curious, and she would be the cause of all those events from the past coming out again. "Do you think you'll be a reporter always?"

"I hope not. One day I hope to run my own newspaper. But until then, I'm learning the ropes, and where better to learn than from here where all the action in the state is? What about you? Are you going to stay with your father's business always? What about getting married and raising a family one day?"

He surprised her with his questioning, but she supposed she'd brought it on by asking about his future. "I don't know. I want to design houses like he does—not so much businesses, but homes." She shrugged. "I'm not sure what the future holds for me."

"Is having a family something you want someday?"

She could only answer truthfully. "It's something I've dreamed about, but—" Charity wasn't ready to say anything more. Maybe she should turn the conversation around to him again. "What about you? Are you going to settle down and have a family of your own one day?"

He flashed her another smile that reached down and turned her heart to pure mush. "Oh, I'm dreaming about it."

❧

Luke and his parents arrived at the Williamsons' before Charity and her parents did, and although many of the city's most eligible young ladies approached him, all gushing over his articles, he had no interest in any of them. He kept watching the entrance to make sure he didn't miss Charity's arrival. He'd told her the truth the evening before. He'd been dreaming about getting married for the first time in his life. What he hadn't told her was *she* was in those dreams. He wondered what it would be like to have a wife like Charity, children with her, and. . .would they have her beautiful red hair? Or those green eyes that turned blue sometimes? Or would they have his dark hair and—

Charity and her parents arrived just then, and Luke was more than a little put out when most of the single males in attendance surrounded her before he could get near. But it didn't stop him from heading in her direction, especially when she kept looking around as if she, too, might be looking for someone. Luke could only hope it was him as her gaze caught his and she smiled.

As he reached her side, Charity said, "Excuse me, gentlemen, but I—"

"She's taking dinner with me tonight." Luke hoped he hadn't overstepped his bounds by his statement, but she did seem to be trying to escape the mob. Luke was more than willing to help her.

"You might know it'd be Johnson who'd capture her attention. Especially now he's made a name for himself in the newspaper world," one man said.

Luke didn't know him, didn't care to, and quickly whisked Charity away. "I hope I didn't take too much for granted by letting them think we'd planned to eat together, but you seemed to be looking to be rescued and I—"

"Came to my rescue. You read me well, and I thank you for it. I'd be glad to have dinner with you if you don't have other plans. You seemed to have attracted your share of attention when we arrived, too." Her green eyes glittered up at him, and he hoped she was as unsettled by the attention he'd been getting as he'd been on seeing her surrounded by so many men.

"Let's just call us a joint rescue team. Will that work?"

She smiled and seemed to relax a bit as she slid her hand through the crook of his arm and rested it on his sleeve. "It will work for me."

It certainly worked for him. He couldn't help but notice the looks of envy many of his friends threw his way, but at least they knew him well enough to stay away. A few of the younger men who were friends of Charity's were cocky enough that they began to approach them, but one look from him, and they turned in another direction, trying to look as if they'd planned to go that way all along.

Something seemed to change between him and Charity that evening, but Luke wasn't sure exactly what. He only knew he liked it.

&

Later that evening, after they returned from the party and while Charity and her mother were alone waiting for her father to join them, the subject of Luke came up.

"Charity, dear, I realize you may not want to talk about this, but how do you feel about Luke Johnson?"

Heat rushed to Charity's cheeks at the unexpected question, and she was sure her mother saw her reaction. "He—Mama, it doesn't really matter how I feel about him. I don't know how he feels about me and. . .even if. . .I'm not sure I can. . ." She stopped and let out a huge sigh. "Mama, I don't know if I can ever be as submissive as the Bible says we should be—as you are to Papa. You know how I can get my mind set on something and—"

"Oh Charity, dear, I am so sorry. We should have talked about this before. Being submissive to the man you love isn't hard at all when you marry one who loves you as much as you love him. When two people truly love each other, they want to please each other, they want to agree on things."

"But what about when you don't agree?"

"Well, the man is the head of the household and we're told to be submissive to him. But your father has always explained those situations where I bowed to his wishes. And if he didn't have a very good reason, he always has taken my thoughts into consideration."

"But not all men are like Papa."

"No. But one who truly loves the Lord and you will be. Because the Bible also tells a man to love his wife as he loves himself. If he loves you that way, it won't be hard for you both to come to an agreement."

Charity shook her head. "I've never seen you and Papa argue about anything."

"I should hope not. But it doesn't mean we haven't on occasion. Most times he's gotten me to see things his way. . . and sometimes, Charity, I've gotten him to come around to my way of thinking. But by the time a decision has been made, we've both agreed to be of one mind going forward on it."

"How will I know that kind of man?"

"I know it sounds trite. But you will know—as long as you let yourself get to know him and let him show you the kind of man he really is. Are we talking about anyone specific?" her mother asked. "Luke Johnson, maybe? Or is this just an in general conversation?"

"Oh. . .more in general than anything. I just. . .I'm not sure anyone can measure up to Papa or Uncle Ben, Mama." There, she gave the excuse she'd always given, and maybe her mother would drop the subject.

"Oh, Charity, Of course one can. As long as you find someone who loves the Lord and wants to do His will and be the kind of husband the Bible tells him to be, you'll be very happy. There are other good men out there besides your father, although I admit he is the best example you could find of the kind of husband you need."

"He is." And maybe Luke was that kind of man. Charity wanted him to be for she knew he'd already claimed a big chunk of her heart. "I'm just not sure I can find a man that good."

"Of course you can, Charity. But you need to be discerning and in prayer about it."

"But what if I fall in love with someone and am sure he's right for me—how can I be as certain I can be good for him?"

"When you truly fall in love, Charity, you'll know. The Lord will make it clear to you. Trust me. He did for your father and me."

Charity prayed her mother was right. She needed some clarity in her life.

≈

As the days passed, it became almost impossible for Charity to deny that her feelings for Luke were growing. He was so considerate of everyone at the boardinghouse—especially Grammy Rose. He always seated her at the table, and he talked to her, giving her his undivided attention, asking her about Guthrie and the run she'd made on her own as her husband had gone to the front of the line.

Just the evening before, he'd got her talking about the run and how she'd come to live at the boardinghouse.

"Why, it was the best thing that ever happened to me after my husband passed away," Grammy had said. "I really didn't know what to do. But then I answered an advertisement for help, and I couldn't believe it when Faith opened the door. She'd been the one to start out the run with me, her and Hope and Matt going it by themselves, too. It was like finding long-lost relatives, and they've been my family ever since. The Lord blessed me greatly that day."

"He blessed us all, Grammy Rose," Hope said.

Grammy loved the attention Luke gave her, and Charity figured one never got too old to enjoy talking to a handsome man. He made sure to talk to the boarders and Hope's children, too. They were all quite impressed to have a reporter living under their roof—especially one making such a good name for himself.

After spending several weekends in the city, Charity decided to stay in Guthrie and was quite pleased when Luke chose not to go to the city either. It pleased her even more when he came down on Sunday morning ready to go to church with the family. Her whole family had been going to the same church since it opened in Guthrie right after the land run, and while Charity loved the church her parents went to in the city, walking into the Guthrie church just felt like home.

There was obvious curiosity about Luke sitting next to her, and she knew she'd be questioned about him later, but for now, she just let herself enjoy this day in the church she grew up in, sitting beside the man who'd begun to mean so much to her.

As always, the minister brought a lesson to take to heart. She felt the Lord was talking to her through the minister's sermon on trust. She needed to put her trust in God for everything—from whether she'd be a good wife, to having the right man enter her life if He meant for her to marry. And if Luke was the man, she needed to trust the Lord would make it plain. . .in His time.

After the service, Charity introduced Luke to the minister. "Luke Johnson, this is Charles Bradley, our minister. He and his wife, Mary, have been here since before I entered this world."

"And we've watched you grow into a beautiful young woman. It's good to have you here today, Charity. I know you go to be with your parents most weekends, but we do miss you when you are gone." He turned to Luke. "It's nice to meet you, Mr. Johnson. I hope you join us again."

"Oh, I'll be sure to when I'm in town on a Sunday. I enjoyed your lesson today."

"Thank you. Your words are music to a minister's ears. I hear you are staying at the boardinghouse. I'm sure everyone has made you feel like you belong there."

"Oh yes, they have." Luke looked down at Charity. "It feels like home now."

Minister Bradley nodded. "I'm sure it does. My wife and I have enjoyed your articles in the paper very much. We're sure hoping Guthrie remains the capital, but we appreciate the fairness with which you've written your articles."

"Why, thank you, sir." Luke chuckled. "Your words are music to *my* ears."

"You are staying for the first picnic of the season, aren't you?"

Luke looked at Charity. "Are we?"

She nodded. "Yes. Didn't you notice the baskets Hope loaded into their auto?"

"No, I'm afraid I didn't. But I'm glad we're staying. I haven't been to a church picnic in a long time."

As they walked away to help Hope and Thomas set out their food, Luke took hold of her elbow. "I like this church."

"So do I." And he'd made it extra special for her today. "I'm glad you came with us."

"Me, too."

Luke enjoyed the whole afternoon. Everyone was friendly and welcomed him like an old friend. Children played games of hide-and-seek and stickball, while some of the men joined them for the three-legged races.

Luke and Matt were partners for the three-legged race while Thomas partnered with his son, but Luke and Matt didn't make it over ten feet before getting tangled up and knocking down Thomas and Seth. Faith, Hope, and Rose were doubled over with laughter by the time they all managed to stand up.

Luke couldn't remember when he'd enjoyed a Sunday afternoon more. Without fail, everyone he talked to recognized him from his newspaper articles. Most were quite forthcoming about what they thought of the upcoming election. And it wasn't good.

ten

After spending Sunday with Charity and her family, and talking to so many who worried about the coming election, Luke realized he hadn't really done the kind of research he'd intended to do to find out how badly Guthrie might be hurt if the capital did get moved to the city. On Monday morning, he waited until most of the regulars cleared out of the Capitol Café before motioning to the owner, Mrs. Lester.

"What can I do for you, Mr. Johnson? You need a refill on your coffee?" the short, rotund woman asked.

"Only if you'll join me for a cup. I'd like to ask you a few questions."

She seemed to size him up before giving a short nod. "Let me get a cup and I'll join you."

In only a few moments she joined him, refilling his cup and pouring one of her own. "Am I going to be in the paper?"

"Do you want to be?"

"Not particularly. Your paper isn't the one I normally read. But I like your articles, so I guess it'd be all right. . . ."

Luke got right to the point. "What do you think will happen to your business—to the town—if the capital is moved to Oklahoma City?"

"I don't really know for sure, but I can't see how I'll be able to stay open with all the legislators gone. They are a major part of my clientele. Without them, I don't know how I'll be able to make a living, and who's going to want to buy me out?"

Luke couldn't answer. Why would anyone buy out a failed business?

"It's not just me. Go talk to any of the business owners in town. A few will survive, but we don't know which ones. We're all worried."

Luke didn't know what to say. From the look on Mrs. Lester's face, nothing he could say would give her hope.

She drained her cup and stood. "Guess I'd better get back to work while I still have customers to see to."

"Thank you for your time, Mrs. Lester. I appreciate it. I hope to write an article that will get your views out there."

"And I hope your boss will let you print it. But I don't hold out much hope it will happen."

Luke didn't either, but he knew he must try.

When he left, he canvassed both sides of the street and found Mrs. Lester's fear universal. Mr. Taylor, the barber; Mr. Ling, who ran the laundry Luke used; and several managers of the larger hotels all worried they'd end up losing their businesses and have to leave Guthrie. It seemed Charity might be right.

He returned to the office and found his two-fingered pecking at the keys on his Underwood was much too slow for the myriad of thoughts he wanted to get across. But he kept at it until he finished the article and was happy with it, hoping with all his heart Mr. Niblack would print it.

He pulled the paper out of the typewriter and took it to Niblack, but the man barely skimmed it before tossing it to the side. "We'll see if we can work it in somewhere."

Luke left the office with the feeling his article might never see the light of day.

⁂

The next day Mr. Niblack sent Luke on the road again, and the rest of the week crawled to Charity's way of thinking. She felt Luke's absence in a way she hadn't expected to. The house she'd grown up in didn't feel quite the same without him.

She fairly jumped at the chance to go out when Lizzy asked her to dinner on Thursday evening. Her friend wanted Charity's help on planning her wedding, which would take place at the end of June.

Lizzy's parents welcomed her like a long-lost daughter, and it felt almost as good as being home with her parents.

"We don't see as much of you as we'd like to, Charity," Lizzy's mother said. "What have you been up to besides work and going to the city on weekends?"

Mr. Barns chuckled. "Seems to me she has plenty to keep a girl busy, dear."

"Yes, I suppose so. How are your mother and father? I so miss them. But I hope they are happy in the city."

"Oh, they are. But they miss everyone here, too. They are fine. Papa is busy trying to persuade people to vote to keep the capital in Guthrie when the elections come around."

"Oh, I am so worried about it all," Mrs. Barns said. "I'm afraid Guthrie will just dry up and blow away and—"

"That isn't going to happen, Mama," Lizzy assured her. "But it certainly isn't going to keep growing unless someone finds gold in the center of town, and I don't think that's going to happen either."

"No, it's not. It will hurt the town, for sure. But as long as there are sick people in town, I'll have a job," Mr. Barns said. "Town will always need pharmacies. But I can see why your father moved to the city. Even though there's enough business to keep Matt busy, there is much more building going on there."

"Yes, there is. Still, I know it will break Papa and Mama's hearts if Guthrie doesn't remain the capital."

Mr. Barns nodded and said, "When you come in and help build a town, you want it to grow and prosper. It'll be a sad day for everyone if the governor is successful in getting the capital moved. I'm glad I didn't vote for him."

Charity wanted to mention her father was thinking of running for governor if the bid to move the capital was successful, but he hadn't made a decision yet, and it wasn't her news to tell until he did.

"Let's talk about something much more exciting than elections," Lizzy said. "I'm ready to talk about my wedding plans."

"Well now, daughter," her father said, "which one is better to talk about is a matter of opinion. I'm not too keen on talking about my only daughter getting married. I think I'll let you ladies discuss it, and I'll go read the newspaper. That young reporter—Luke Johnson, I believe his name is—has written some good articles about the fight to keep the capital here. Seems your papa started something in the city that's spreading all over the state, Charity."

"Mr. Johnson is the man who ran into the back of Charity's auto, Papa. And he lives at the boardinghouse," Lizzy said.

"He did? And he does?" Mr. Barns asked.

"Yes, sir. Only he hasn't been around much this week. He's out getting material for those articles."

"Well, he's doing a fine job. I'm sure Niblack is glad he's working for him and not some other paper. . .although, I'm quite surprised he's giving him as much freedom as he is with his articles. I think it may be he's trying to gain a new readership that will buy the paper to read Mr. Johnson's articles and then try to sway them with his own editorials."

"I think you are right, Mr. Barns." Charity felt a certain pride in knowing Luke and in having her father be the one to help him in his career. For Gabe Logan was known and respected by all who knew him, and Mr. Niblack must have been impressed her father agreed to an interview with Luke. The fact that Luke managed to get the interview was something no one else had done in a long while. Still, it bothered her that Luke worked for the *Daily Leader*, which was so openly for moving the capital. So far Luke had been fair and honest in his articles, but Charity wondered how much longer his paper would let him continue to, or when they were going to demand he take their side in the way he wrote. What would Luke do then?

Mr. Barns got up from the table and excused himself. "I'll let you ladies plan all you want. I'm going to catch up on my news."

They made quick work of clearing the table, but Mrs. Barns shooed them out of the kitchen. "You two go ahead and start looking through Lizzy's magazines, and I'll get the kitchen cleaned up. Then I'll come see what you've got left to pick from."

"Oh no, Mrs. Barns. We can help you clean up. You should be the one helping Lizzy decide these things and—"

"Charity, dear, you know how long it takes Lizzy to make a decision. I will most likely be through cleaning up long before it's come down to the final one. Besides, we've been discussing dresses for weeks now. If you can just help her weed out the things she's not thrilled with, you'd be helping me more than cleaning my kitchen would."

Charity didn't feel right leaving Lizzy's mother to do all the work. "But—"

"She means it, Charity. She's the one who suggested I ask you to dinner tonight to help."

Everyone knew Lizzy had a hard time making decisions. That's why it came as such a surprise when she'd set a date to get married. But come to find out, Edward had insisted on the date, and as for the decision to marry him. . .well, Lizzy always said they'd decided to marry each other long before they were old enough to worry about decision making.

"All right. Let's go look over your magazines, Lizzy. Surely there is one pattern you love the very best."

For the next two hours they pored over fashion plates from the year before to the latest of *Harper's Bazaar* and *Vogue* magazines. Charity's favorite was a gown of white lace and chiffon, but Lizzy leaned toward more ruffles and silk, so Charity quickly focused her on what her friend truly loved and told her to forget the rest. There was no need to look at the ones Charity liked—it wasn't as if she had wedding plans after all. But Charity couldn't help feeling a little envious of her friend.

What was happening to her? Just a few weeks ago, she'd

loved her life. Loved everything about it. Loved that she could call both Guthrie and Oklahoma City home. Loved earning her own money, feeling independent and, up until lately, being fully capable of making decisions for herself. She'd been glad she wasn't attached to any of the young men she knew and didn't pine for one. But everything changed the day Luke ran into the back of her auto, and now her life seemed to have turned upside down.

&

Charity tried not to show how disappointed she was Luke still wasn't back by the time she got home from Lizzy's. Did he intend to come back to Guthrie at all this week? His last article came from Stillwater, but she had no idea where he was now. She only knew she missed him very much.

On Friday Charity still hadn't decided whether to go to the city for the weekend or stay in Guthrie. She kept looking for Luke to show up and held her breath each time the door opened. But he never came through it.

All afternoon she went back and forth over what to do. One minute she thought she'd stay in Guthrie, and the next she thought it'd be better if she went home—especially if Luke didn't come back for the weekend. Then she became upset with herself for even taking into consideration what he might do.

In the end, a call from her father made her mind up.

Matt answered the telephone and motioned to her. He held his hand over the receiver and whispered. "It's your papa, and he sounds upset."

She'd no more than said hello before she learned Matt's instinct was correct.

"Charity, I've got bad news, dear. Your mama came downstairs this morning with some clothing she wanted to donate to charity, but she missed the last step on the stairs leading into the kitchen, and—"

"Oh no! Papa is she all right?"

"Well, no. She landed on her arm and broke it. The doctor has set it, and I've hired a maid to help out, but she's in a lot of pain. I want some family here with her when I can't be. And I'm scheduled to do some traveling next week. But there's no way I'll leave her without—"

"I'll come right away, Papa."

"I knew you would. But you won't be able to stay indefinitely—Matt needs you there, too. I thought maybe you could bring Rose, if she's willing to come for a while to keep your mother company."

"Oh, I'm sure she will be. I'll ask and ring you back right away."

"Thank you, dear."

"Give Mama my love!"

Charity ran over to the boardinghouse, told her grandmother what had happened, and asked if she could go to the city with her that afternoon. Just as she'd expected, Grammy didn't hesitate for a minute.

"Oh, of course I'll go. It's been too long since I've spent any time with your mother and father. Is she in a lot of pain?" Worry lines creased Grammy Rose's forehead.

Tears came to Charity's eyes as she remembered the concern in her father's voice. "Papa says she is. And you know how he hates to see any of us hurting."

Grammy Rose nodded. "Oh yes I do. Especially if he can't

do anything to make it better right away. I'll go get my bags packed."

She hurried out of the kitchen, and Charity turned to Hope. "Papa did sound worried. I might stay an extra day or so, depending on how bad Mama is feeling. You know we won't let Grammy do too much. I think Papa just wants her there to boost Mama's morale and keep her company while he's gone."

"I can understand why he would. I'm glad Grammy is going, too. She'll be great company for Aunt Faith, and she'll calm your papa down as well. Besides, it will be good for her. She needs to get away once in a while. I think it does her good to feel needed. Of course she is, but she doesn't always feel that way with us trying to make things easy on her. She says life is easier than she ever expected before she came to live with us all, and the least she can do is help out."

"Well, she'll sure be helping out by being there for Mama."

"I made two cakes this afternoon. I'll send one with you."

"You don't have to, Hope."

"I know. But right now it's all I can do for Aunt Faith, besides pray."

"And you know praying is the most important thing, and we'll be counting on those prayers. But"—she looked at the three-layer chocolate cake on the counter—"I'll take the cake, too."

"Good." Hope hugged her. "It's your mother's recipe."

"She'll be touched you sent it. I'd better go telephone Papa and tell him we'll be on our way, soon as we get packed."

As soon as she hung up from talking to her father, she turned to go upstairs and get packed. But the front door opened just then, and Luke walked in.

"Charity! I didn't expect to see you yet. Have you quit work for today?"

"I have—well, I suppose I'd best go let Matt know I have. Mama's suffered an accident, and Grammy Rose and I are going to the city."

"Oh no. Is she hurt badly?"

Charity's emotions warred with worry over her mother and the joy she felt at seeing Luke. "She broke her arm, and Papa says she's in a lot of pain."

"I'm so sorry. If my auto were big enough, I'd be glad to drive you both there."

"I. . ." Charity would like nothing more than to have him do just that. She did feel a bit shaky. "I'd let you drive us in my auto, but I'm sure you don't want to get back on the road again."

"I'm going to the city anyway, Charity. Then I'll be heading to Shawnee next week. I'd be more than glad to take you. I can take the train back home if you aren't ready to come when I need to get back. Besides, I haven't seen you in forever it seems. I'm sure you are upset about your mother. Please, let me drive you and Miss Rose."

It sounded as if he'd missed her, too, and that settled it for Charity. "You know, if you are sure, I'd appreciate your driving us. I am a little unsettled at Papa's news."

"Good. I'm glad I can do something to help you." His smile did those funny things to her heart. It kind of swelled and turned all warm and melty inside. "When did you want to leave?"

"Would sometime in the next hour be all right with you?"

"That's plenty of time for me to get ready. I'll go repack and be ready anytime you are. And I'll be glad to take Miss Rose's and your bags out to the car."

"Thank you, Luke. I'll go let her know."

She hurried back to her grandmother's room to let her know and then to let Hope know Luke was back but wouldn't be staying long. She made a quick phone call to Matt to let him know her plans, and as she headed up the stairs to do her own packing, she sent up a silent thank-you to the Lord for bringing Luke back. She didn't know why, but she felt a kind of comfort that he was back in town and she would get to see him, if only on the drive to the city.

eleven

The trip from Guthrie to Oklahoma City was very quiet. Both Charity and her grandmother seemed lost in their thoughts, and Luke didn't know what to say so he prayed Mrs. Logan would be all right. He thought back to his last conversation with his boss. Niblack had decided not to use the article that meant so much to Luke, and while it came as no surprise, it'd been a huge disappointment to him.

"You know this isn't the kind of article the governor wants me to run, Luke." Mr. Niblack handed the paper back to him. "Maybe if you revise it so it isn't so obvious you sympathize with these people—"

"Mr. Niblack, I made sure not to take sides. I only reported what I was told and—"

"We aren't printing it, Johnson. And I hope the next article you turn in is more in line with what we've been getting from you."

Remembering those words, Luke shook his head. He supposed that since he hadn't given the opposing view, his boss was right. It might have seemed slanted. But it was the overall feeling of the people of Guthrie, and he felt it was time he told their story. If he worked for the *State Capitol*, the article would have already made the front page... something to think about while he was on the road.

He turned off the highway to the street leading to the

Logans' home. "We're nearly at your home now, Charity. No sense in you driving me home and then having to come back. I know you are eager to see your mother. I'll just drive to your home and telephone my father to come pick me up."

"I don't mind taking you to your parents'," Charity said. "But I would like to stop and check on Mama first."

"And I'd be disappointed in you if you didn't. But Papa will be glad to pick me up, or I'll hire a hack to come get me. Your parents need you." Luke could see the worry in her eyes, and he wanted to help in any way he could. "I hope you know my family and I will be glad to help in any way we can."

"Thank you, Luke. I'll be sure to tell Papa."

Luke pulled into the long drive leading to her parents' home and stopped the auto. He quickly ran around and helped Grammy Rose out of the touring auto.

"I'd forgotten how big and beautiful this home is," Rose said as she gripped her bag and took the arm Luke offered her. He turned to Charity. "I'll bring in your bags soon as I get Miss Rose inside."

"Thank you." When the door opened and her father stepped outside, she hurried on ahead and into his waiting arms.

"The doctor gave her something for the pain, and she's feeling a little better now," Luke heard him say. "She said the setting of it hurt the most, and it's not so bad now. But Doc says she's going to be in pain for several days."

"Is she in your room?" Charity asked.

"For now. You know how she is. I didn't tell her you and Rose were coming. She would have insisted on being right here to greet you. And Mr. Johnson, too, of course." Mr.

Logan held out his hand to Luke.

"Hello, sir."

"Thank you for driving Charity in, Luke. I worried about her driving herself after the news I gave her."

"You're welcome, sir. I'd planned on coming over anyway, and it seemed a good idea. I'd like to telephone my father and ask him to pick me up, if it's all right."

"Certainly. I'll be glad to take you home myself now that Charity and Rose are here to stay with Faith."

"Oh no, sir. I wouldn't think of having you leave your family at a time like this. I'll be praying Mrs. Logan heals completely and quickly."

They all entered the huge foyer, and Charity turned to him. "Luke, thank you so much for driving in with us. It helped to take the worry off our minds. I hope your trip to Shawnee is successful for you."

"Thank you for allowing me to drive you in, Charity. If you need anything at all, please don't hesitate to telephone my parents. And when I get back, I will check and see if there is anything I can do."

"Thank you. I'm going to look in on Mama now." Charity turned, and she and her grandmother hurried away.

"The telephone is in my office, Luke. Feel free to use it while I go have some iced tea brought in to us."

"Thank you, sir. But don't worry about me. I can wait outside until my father gets here."

"Nonsense. I'll be right back."

"Yes, sir. If I'm not here, I'll be out bringing in the rest of the ladies' baggage."

"Thank you."

Luke quickly put a call through to his father, who said he'd be there as soon as he could. Then he went out and brought in the ladies' bags. Mr. Logan came back into the foyer just as Luke came inside.

"Put them down there, son. I'll get them to the right rooms later. Come on in my office, and we'll have some tea while we wait for your father."

He motioned for Luke to take a chair by the fireplace and handed him a glass of iced tea before taking one for himself from the tray that had been brought into the room. Then he took the other chair flanking the fireplace. "Faith seemed to relax once she saw Charity and Rose, so now maybe I can calm down a little, too. It's awful hard for me to see my women in pain."

The thought of Charity hurting sent a shiver through Luke, and the memory of the worry in her eyes made him feel he could understand. "It has to be very difficult to see a loved one hurting and not be able to make it better."

"It is. My job is to look after them, protect them, and keep them safe. But some things we simply aren't in control of."

"Yes, sir." Luke didn't really think Mr. Logan expected him to say much. He sensed Charity's father needed to talk.

Mr. Logan took a long sip of his iced tea and nodded. "And it's a good reminder of who is in charge. Seems that's when we have to go to the Lord for help in dealing with it all. I'm just thankful Faith wasn't hurt any worse—she could have missed the top stair instead of the last one."

"That would have been horrible," Luke agreed. He didn't even want to think about it.

"So, Charity mentioned you are going to Shawnee?"

"Yes, sir. Mr. Niblack liked my articles on you so well and your idea of fighting to keep Guthrie the capital, he's asked me to see what the citizens in other towns in the state are doing. And it appears Shawnee is going to be on the ballot."

"Doesn't surprise me," Mr. Logan said. "Rumor here is Haskell wanted to get Shawnee on the ballot to take votes away from Guthrie. I've enjoyed reading your articles. . . as have many of my friends."

"Mr. Niblack wouldn't have given me this assignment if not for you and the interview you gave me, Mr. Logan. I can't thank you enough for talking to me."

"You are a good reporter, Luke. Niblack would have sat up and taken notice without me. I'll admit I wish you were writing for the *State Capitol*—their views are much more in line with my way of thinking. But you've been fair, and if I can help you in any way, give you names you might want to contact, you let me know."

"Why thank you, sir." Luke had begun to wish he did work for the other paper.

"In fact, let me write down a few names of people you might want to look up in Shawnee." Mr. Logan got up and went to his desk and began writing on a notepad. He handed Luke a list of at least fifteen names in Shawnee. "These should get you started."

"I can't tell you how much this means to me, sir." Luke folded the paper and put it in his shirt pocket.

"I'm rarely wrong in reading people, Luke. You are a good reporter. One who tells the truth and cares what happens to this state. It comes through in your writing, whether you realize it or not—and you've been careful not to come out for either side. This state needs more reporters like you."

"Why, thank you, sir. I must confess, at first I didn't understand why so many were against moving the capital. But as I've come to know more people in Guthrie and all over the state, I think I understand your cause better."

"There's something I'd like to—" A knock on the front door interrupted Mr. Logan. "That's probably your father now."

Luke sighed as his host went to the door. His father never did have great timing, and it appeared that hadn't changed. Luke followed Mr. Logan to greet his father, wishing he'd have been just a little late coming to pick him up. He really wanted to know what Charity's father had been about to say.

twelve

When Luke got back to the city from Shawnee, he borrowed his father's auto and stopped by to see how Mrs. Logan was doing—and to get a glimpse of Charity. It was becoming exceedingly difficult to keep her out of his mind, and when she opened the door to him, his chest tightened at the look in her eyes. She seemed almost glad to see him.

"I just got back into town and wanted to see how things are going. How is your mother doing?"

"She's healing well, Doc says, and it's a good thing because we can't keep her down." Charity ushered him into the foyer. "But Papa has to be out of town for several days the first part of the week, and neither of us wants to leave her and Grammy Rose alone yet."

"So you won't be returning tomorrow?" Disappointment settled heavy in his heart.

"No. I'm sorry I won't be able to give you a ride back."

"Oh, don't worry about it. I understand completely why you are staying. I'll just take the train back." While he understood why Charity was staying over, he'd be glad when she returned to Guthrie. Much as he liked Guthrie, it wasn't quite as appealing when she wasn't there.

Charity led him to the back parlor where her parents and grandmother were gathered. They all welcomed him as if he were a long-lost friend. Mrs. Logan seemed to be doing much better than he'd expected. So much so they asked him to stay for lunch, and Luke wasn't about to turn down a chance to spend more time with Charity, especially when he didn't know for sure when he'd see her again.

"Why, thank you. I'd love to join you, if you are sure it's no bother."

"Not at all," Mrs. Logan said. "We always try to prepare extra, just in case someone stops by."

Charity explained why he'd stopped by.

"That means you don't have a ride back, though, doesn't it?" her father asked.

"Oh, it's no problem. I've taken the train many times." But none of those times were as enjoyable as the ride with Charity, and he knew he'd be thinking about the trip they'd shared all the way home.

"No need for that, Luke. I'm going to go to Guthrie in the morning to discuss a few things with Matt before I go on. I'll be more than happy to give you a ride."

"Why thank you, sir. I'll take you up on your offer if you're sure it's not an imposition. I've a few more questions I'd like to ask you, and we could talk on the way to Guthrie."

"Sounds good to me, son." They made arrangements for Luke's father to bring him over to the Logans' the next morning, and Luke hoped he'd get to at least tell Charity good-bye.

When the cook announced lunch was served, he was pleased to be shown to the small family dinning room and asked to take a seat between Charity and her grandmother.

Conversation flowed easily. They talked about all manner of things from the weather they'd been having to the elections and the upcoming Decoration Day party the Logans were hosting.

"It's actually on the Saturday before Decoration Day, and of course you and your parents are invited. I hadn't planned on having my arm in a sling for it, but no matter. I'm quite looking forward to it," Mrs. Logan said. "And I'm glad Rose and Charity are here to help me with the final decisions."

Luke was glad he'd been invited, but he couldn't tell how Charity felt about it. She seemed quieter than usual, and he hoped she wasn't upset with him for accepting her parents' invitation.

He and Charity didn't have an opportunity to have a private conversation until he left, but he was pleased when she walked him out to his auto.

"Thank you again for checking on Mama."

"I'm glad she's doing better. I understand why you need to stay, but I'll miss you."

A delicate pink crept up her neck and cheeks, and her eyes turned the now familiar deep shade of green-blue he loved. "Thank you. I—" She caught her breath as Luke reached out and touched her chin.

Luke couldn't resist the urge to tip her chin up so he could look into those beautiful eyes once more before he left. He felt he could drown in them—and almost did before he forced himself to lower his hand and take a step back. He let out a deep breath and cranked his father's auto before jumping into the driver's seat. "You take care, and I'll see you when you get back to Guthrie."

"Be careful on your way back." Charity smiled. "And don't stop for any old fox in the road either."

Luke threw back his head and laughed. "I'll be sure not to. I hope to see you soon."

She gave a little wave, and he did the same before he took off. He'd come close to kissing her. Right there in the broad daylight. . .just outside her parents' home. That would have cost him for sure.

&

Luke was glad to ride back to Guthrie with Charity's father, only this time he wasn't looking for a story. He just wanted to get to know the man better. Luke did hope Mr. Logan would get around to telling him whatever he'd started to say the day his father had picked him up, but it wasn't until after they'd discussed the weather, Mrs. Logan's recovery, and the plans for his parents' home that the subject came up.

"Luke, I've been meaning to ask—I suppose because my wife has been urging me to find out—what do you know about my past?"

"Your past, sir?"

Mr. Logan glanced over at him and nodded. "In all your research for your articles, I'm sure you've come across a lot of information."

Luke had to tell the truth. "I'm not sure what I've heard is true, but I've been told you spent some time in jail, sir."

"I did. I started to tell you about it the day you brought Charity and Rose home, but it wasn't the time. Do you know anything more?"

"I heard your fiancée was killed in the middle of a bank robbery, and you went after the man."

Gabe Logan never took his eyes off the highway. "What you've heard is true and to my shame, I did track him down.

I should have let the law handle it from the beginning. But I was so—" he shook his head and sighed. "I was grief stricken, and I thought I could avenge her death instead of trusting the Lord to take care of it."

"Yes, sir. I can imagine how you might want to do that."

"I was wrong, but I did find him. He shot at me; I shot back and hit him in the leg. When I took him in, they put me in jail along with him until it could all be sorted out. Rumor had it I'd tried to rob the bank and. . .it took several months to get the truth out."

Luke hadn't been told about Mr. Logan being suspected of robbing the bank, but he couldn't imagine how the rumor ever came about. "I heard you were pardoned."

Charity's father nodded. "And I asked the Lord's forgiveness for going after the man in the first place. He forgave me right off, but it took a little longer for me to forgive myself."

Luke nodded. Gabe Logan was that kind of man—one who turned his life over to the Lord. The kind Luke aspired to be. "I'm sorry you went through so much—"

"If you knew about this, why didn't you mention it to me or Charity?"

"I didn't want to bring you or your family more pain by asking about it, sir. You were pardoned, and it happened a long time ago. Why bring it out now?"

"I'd think your paper might want to make something of it, should I decide to run for governor—maybe to try and get me not to run."

"They very well might. But I won't be the one writing an article about it, sir. I give you my word."

"That's all I need to know. Charity does know about it all.

We told her when we felt she was old enough to know, but I think she's worried it might all come out again one day."

"Not through me, sir," Luke reiterated.

"That eases my mind, and it will relieve Charity's mother a great deal."

They were both silent until Mr. Logan turned into the drive between his office and the boardinghouse. They got out and shook hands. "Thank you for the ride in, sir."

"Thank you for bringing Charity and Rose to us. See you soon, I imagine?"

"I hope so, sir."

Luke headed to the boardinghouse while Mr. Logan strode to his office.

He liked Charity's father a lot, and there was no way he would intentionally hurt him or his family—especially his daughter.

With Charity in the city, the next week was one of loneliest Luke could ever remember, and after talking to her father, he began to worry Charity's fear might come true. He would not be the one to bring up her father's past, but someone else might. He could only pray it didn't happen. He kept busy writing his articles about all the efforts being put forth by those citizens who wanted to keep the capital in Guthrie and about the three cities that would be on the ballot, but his mind kept straying to Charity and wondering when she would return.

He took comfort in knowing he would see her when she did come home—but somehow meals weren't the same as when she was sitting next to him. Mornings weren't the same if he didn't see her, and the evenings seemed twice as long—

even if he did join the other boarders for a game of cards or charades in the parlor a time or two.

Luke just plain missed Charity's presence and could no longer deny he loved her, had begun to think of a future with her. He made up his mind if she wasn't home by the weekend, he'd be going back to the city. He didn't think he could wait another week to see her.

He wondered how she spent her time now that her mother was feeling better—just that evening Hope told everyone her aunt was healing quickly and doing well. Still, Charity hadn't come home, and Luke was sure those young men who'd surrounded her the night of the Williamsons' party would be calling on her once they knew she was in town caring for her mother. And even though she hadn't seemed interested in any of them, it didn't mean she wasn't or—

The front door opened, and he looked up from the food he'd been pushing around on his plate to see Charity standing in the doorway.

Hope jumped up and gave her a hug. "I'd begun to think you were going to stay in the city forever! You're just in time for supper."

Happiness hammered in his chest as Charity walked toward her empty seat. All the men at the table stood until Luke seated Charity in her chair next to his. As he pushed the chair under the table, he bent and whispered for her ears alone, "I'm glad you're back. I've missed you."

He watched the color of her eyes deepen and a blush steal up her neck, but she didn't have time to reply as everyone began asking about her mother and Rose. He didn't mind. Charity was home, and finally, everything felt right.

❧

When Luke looked up to see her standing in the dining-room doorway, the smile on his face reached all the way into her heart, and it was all Charity could do not to run into his arms. She'd missed him during all this time with him on the road and then her in the city. There was no more denying it. She'd fallen in love with the man. Whether she should or not, it seemed her heart had made the choice to let him in to stay, even if her mind still warned, *be careful; be on guard.*

Her heart had dipped into her stomach when he'd said he missed her, and she was sure Hope wasn't the only one to notice the hurried whisper. Hope flashed a grin at Charity when Luke wasn't looking.

Charity's mother and Rose had insisted she go on back to Guthrie once her father returned home, and she suspected they were trying to do a little matchmaking by getting her and Luke back in the same place.

"You need to give that young man a chance, Charity," Grammy Rose had said just that morning. "I know how he looks at you. He's a good man and—"

"I know, Grammy. I'm just not sure I—"

"Take your time, dear," her mother said. "But know I am praying you don't miss recognizing the person the Lord brings into your life. Maybe it's time to leave things in His hands."

After the talk they'd shared the night of the party, Charity was sure her mother knew she was leery of getting married on many levels, but she didn't go into it with Grammy Rose there, and Charity wasn't sure she'd even talked to her father about it. But it was apparent Mama wanted Charity to find someone or to at least be able to recognize God's will for her. And Charity wanted the same thing.

Charity thought things over all the way home, her foot heavy on the gas peddle. She'd never wanted to get back to Guthrie so fast. Normally she let herself enjoy the scenery, but today she barely noticed that red, yellow, and purple wildflowers rippled in the breeze beside the roadside and that the fruit trees were in full bloom. All she'd wanted was to get back to the boardinghouse. And if Luke had still been out of town, she'd have been ready to call the paper and find out where Niblack had sent him this time.

She'd been thinking of Luke ever since he'd stopped by and had lunch with her family. For a moment, just before he'd left that day, she thought he might kiss her. The fact that she'd held her breath waiting for him to. . .wanting him to kiss her, told her more than anything else about her feelings for him.

Now as she sat beside him, aware of every movement he made—from whispering in her ear the very words she wanted to hear, to cutting his meat or buttering a roll, to stealing glances she returned—Charity wondered if he'd ever get close to kissing her again.

thirteen

Something seemed different since Charity had returned to Guthrie. She didn't know if it was with her or Luke—or both of them—but she was afraid to put a name to it. All she knew was she was happiest when they were together, and when they weren't, he was all she thought about. Half the time she felt as if she were riding the roller coaster at Delmar Gardens in the city—up, down, level, up, down, level, and up again, each time Luke smiled at her.

She found it difficult to focus, and it showed.

"Charity, I don't know where your mind is this week, but this is the third mistake I've found in the books today." Matt opened the ledger to show her where she'd subtracted instead of adding several figures.

"Oh Matt, I'm sorry. I admit, I've found it hard to concentrate the past few days."

"I suppose it's normal with your mother breaking her arm and you having to be in the city for over two weeks. At least the remedy to your mistakes is in our favor. But why don't you take the rest of the afternoon off? Call Lizzy and go get a cup of tea or something? Maybe you just need to relax a little."

"Oh Matt, what a great idea! I'll telephone her now and find out if she can take a break this afternoon." He was a great cousin, giving her an excuse for being so muddle-minded and then a break on top of it.

Lizzy was free the whole afternoon. She wouldn't be working after she married—her husband-to-be didn't want her to—and so she only worked part-time now, just until they could find a replacement for her. She quickly agreed to meet Charity at the Capitol Café.

"Thanks, Matt. I'll try really hard not to make any mistakes tomorrow."

"I'm going to count on it," he said with an exaggerated growl. "See you in the morning."

Charity plucked her hat off the hat rack by the door and quickly pinned it on top of her hair. She didn't think Matt would change his mind, but she was getting out of the office before he had second thoughts. She grabbed her bag and gave him a wave. "See you in the morning."

This time Lizzy was waiting on her, and Charity had never seen her look happier. She dropped down in the seat across from her friend. "You fairly glow, Lizzy. Are you excited?"

"Oh, ever so much! I can't believe I'll be married in just over a month. To think, me, a married woman!"

"I know. I am so happy for you." And Charity meant it. But along with being happy for Lizzy came a longing to be as happy herself.

"Oh look, Charity, there's Luke Johnson crossing the street. I bet he's coming in here. He certainly has made a name for himself with his reporting, hasn't he?"

Charity's heart skipped a beat and then two as Luke headed to the café. He must not have noticed her auto parked outside or just assumed it was someone else's, because he didn't look around when he entered the café. Instead he headed to the back corner where several legislators were gathered at two tables.

It looked to Charity like they were mostly those who would like to see the capital moved, and for the first time in a while, her suspicions about Luke and what side he fell on in the capital debate rose up again. Right behind those came her fear of his career. He could hurt her father in the future if he found out about Papa's past, especially if his political beliefs were on the opposing side.

"Charity? Are you all right?" Lizzy asked.

Charity realized she'd been staring into her teacup. "I'm sorry, Lizzy. I've been having a problem concentrating lately. That's why Matt let me off for the afternoon. I made one too many mistakes in the ledger."

"It's understandable you'd be a little scatterbrained with all you've had going on. For a moment, I thought maybe that handsome Luke Johnson might have something to do with your woolgathering."

"Oh Lizzy, you don't give up, do you?"

"You certainly would make a nice-looking couple, Charity. And just think what beautiful babies you'd have—"

"Lizzy!" Charity looked around to see who might have heard her friend, and it was then Luke seemed to notice her. His gaze caught hers, and for a moment she forgot to breathe. He excused himself from his table companions and headed over their way.

"Charity, I didn't expect to find you here. What a pleasant surprise!" He nodded in Lizzy's direction. "Hello, Miss Barns. How are you both this fine afternoon?"

"I'm quite well," Lizzy answered. "But Charity is having a

hard time concentrating today. Matt finally suggested she get a cup of tea."

Sometimes her friend was entirely too open with everyone. Charity glared at Lizzy, but her friend was too busy looking at Luke to notice.

He pulled out a chair and sat down. "Are you all right, Charity? You haven't had bad news about your mother or anything, have you?"

His concern touched her heart, and she realized how badly she wanted to trust this man. "Mama is fine and so am I. I'm just finding it hard to get back into my routine. Thank you for asking."

"You've been dealing with a lot lately. I suppose I'd best get back to work, but. . .I'll see you at supper. Right, Charity?"

There was the smile again. The one she couldn't keep from responding to. "Yes, I'll be there."

"Good. See you then. Nice to see you again, Miss Barns." Luke stood, gave a small salute, and turned to leave.

Lizzy stared after him as he walked out the door. "I have just one question for you, Charity."

"Oh?"

"Are you blind or what? Luke Johnson is sweet on you, and if you don't want to see someone else in this town beat you to him, you might think about letting him know you feel the same way about him."

"How do you know how I—"

"I'm not blind, my friend. And I've known you much too long not to know you feel something for Luke Johnson."

It seemed everyone she knew could tell how she felt about Luke—could he see it, too?

&

It was a beautiful May evening, and after supper Luke finally got up the nerve to ask Charity to take a walk down by Cottonwood Creek. For a moment, he thought she might refuse him, but then she smiled and nodded.

"I'd love to. Just let me help with the dishes first, and I'll meet you on the front porch."

"I'll wait for you there."

Most of the boarders disappeared after the meal, and he supposed they'd gone out, too. It was a treat to have the porch swing to himself for a change. He sat down and put it in motion, wishing Charity were there to share it with him. He'd daydreamed many a time about sitting here with her. She came outside after only about half an hour. He stood and steadied the swing. "That didn't take long."

"Oh we have it down to an art. Hope has brought up both of her children to know how to do dishes, so it's mostly just a matter of clearing the table and putting things up."

"Her children are very well behaved. I enjoy being around them a lot."

"They are great. But of course I'm partial."

They moved down the steps of one accord, and she let Luke pull her hand through his arm as they went down the walk. "I can drive us if you'd rather—"

"Oh no, I prefer walking. The weather has been wonderful this week."

They strolled down the street and crossed over and down until they came to the banks of the Cottonwood. Several people were out in boats—one couple reminding him of the evening he'd wanted to kiss Charity, only the fear of winding up in the creek had stopped him. Others were out rowing, too, and a few young boys were fishing. Several other couples were walking along the bank as he and Charity were, except they were obviously sweethearts. They were holding hands and leaning their heads close to talk to each other.

Luke stopped at a cottonwood tree, its fresh new leaves shading the bench underneath it. "Would you like to sit a few minutes?"

"Yes, I would." She sat down, and he took a seat beside her. A light breeze blew across them, bringing with it the delicate scent he'd come to associate with Charity. It reminded him of the lilac bush outside his bedroom window at his parents' home.

Together they watched twilight spread across the evening sky, blue-black to deep azure to a blazing orange-and-yellow sunset. Then the sunset disappeared. The blue-black turned darker, and stars dotted the sky. Lights came on in the homes near the creek, and frogs began to croak. Luke could think of nothing better than sharing this time of day with Charity.

"This is my favorite—" They both laughed as they spoke the words at the same time. Luke gazed into Charity's eyes and smiled as they finished together: "Time of day."

It was all he could do to keep from taking her in his arms and kissing her—something he'd thought often about ever since the day he'd stopped by her parents' home. His gaze rested on her lips, and—

She jumped up so suddenly he wondered if she could read his thoughts.

"I suppose we should get back to the boardinghouse," Charity said, brushing at her skirt as if she'd just gotten up from the supper table and there were crumbs on it.

She didn't look at him as he pulled her hand through his arm once more, and Luke wondered—no, hoped it might be because she'd wanted him to kiss her, too. "I wish we could stay awhile, but of course, Hope will probably be worrying about you as it is."

"Why would she worry? I'm sure she believes no harm could come to me as long as I'm with you. Besides, I've been walking down here all my life."

She was safe with him; he'd protect her with his life so no harm came to her. And kissing her could well be more harmful to him than to her. For if she didn't respond, or if she slapped his face, he'd be the one hurt. He didn't know if he could take that kind of rejection from the woman he'd come to love. But one day soon, he was going to have to find out how she felt about him.

Not sure what to say next, Luke decided to change the subject. "Have you heard from your parents today? How is your mother doing?"

"I'm sure she's doing well; she's busy making all kinds of plans for the Decoration Day party. Are you going to be able to come?"

"Oh, yes. I wouldn't miss it. Would you like to ride in with me?"

"I suppose there's no reason to take my auto since everyone is going. Well, the boarders are going to have to fend for themselves that day, but they've all made plans and don't mind. And there's no sense in you having to make the ride by yourself. So yes, I'd like to ride in with you."

He might not kiss her, but he couldn't resist squeezing her

hand as they arrived back at the boardinghouse. "Good. I'm looking forward to it."

&

Luke spent the rest of the evening wondering if he should let Charity know he knew about her father's past—and he'd never hurt her by writing an article on it. On the one hand, he wanted her to know, but on the other, he didn't want to hurt her by bringing it up. Maybe her father would tell her they'd talked about it.

Lately he'd been wondering if he should quit working for the *Daily Leader*. When he'd begun working there, he hadn't understood all the fuss about where the capital was located. But after living in Guthrie, getting to know the citizens, finding out how badly the town would be hurt if the capital wasn't there, he'd found it more than a little difficult to work for a paper whose owner stood for the opposite of what he'd come to believe.

He tossed and turned most of the night, got up, and paced the floor before finally taking his concerns to the only One who could truly help him. "Dear Lord, please guide me in the next few days to know what to do. To know if I should tell Charity I know about her father, to help me decide what to do about my job. And most especially, Lord, please help me to know when to tell Charity how I feel about her— or if I should tell her at all. I don't think I've ever been quite so confused in my life. Please help me to know what to do. In Jesus' name I pray, Amen."

Only then did he finally drift off to sleep. But when he awakened the next morning, he felt refreshed and eager to get on with the day. As he entered the Capitol Café, he realized the Lord moved extra fast to assure him he was on the right path. Luke found his boss sitting at a table by himself, and he took the opportunity to approach him.

"May I join you, sir?"

Mr. Niblack motioned to the seat across from him and nodded as he swallowed the biscuit and gravy he'd just taken a bite of.

Luke pulled out the chair and sat down. He knew what he was going to do, and he was confident the Lord would be at his side, come what may.

fourteen

Luke showed up at the boardinghouse a little later than usual, but he seemed in a very good mood when they set out for the city. The trip made Charity realize how much she liked traveling with Luke. It was during those drives that they talked most easily with one another. Something about being in the confines of an automobile with him seemed to make it easier to talk. Perhaps it was because no one else was there, no one was listening, and they could talk about anything they wanted to. But today Luke seemed quieter than usual, although he seemed to be in a good mood.

She hated to see him leave after he dropped her off at her parents', but she comforted herself with the knowledge she'd see him the next night at the party her parents were hosting and then at church on Sunday. All she knew about Decoration Day on Monday was that they'd be picnicking on the North Canadian after a parade downtown. Oklahoma was still so young its cemeteries didn't hold those who'd died in the Civil War, whose graves were decorated with flowers on the day, but everyone's thoughts would be on those who'd died fighting for this country.

Uncle Ben and Aunt Samantha, along with Hope and her family, came in late that night, and they enjoyed a wonderful family get-together. They talked late into the night, catching up with each other and discussing the upcoming election and the future of the state.

Charity found she missed Luke, and she wondered what sharing a family evening with him as her husband would be like, but she quickly banished the thought. Luke hadn't given her reason to think he might have the same kind of thoughts. Still, she couldn't wait to see him the next evening.

The Saturday of the long weekend dawned bright and beautiful, if a bit breezy. Family pitched in everywhere, helping to set things up. The terrace was full of round tables, their centerpiece lanterns waiting to be lit.

Charity arranged her mother and grandmother's hair and then went to dress herself. She'd chosen a princess dress of pale-green batiste generously trimmed in val lace with a princess panel in the front made of fine tucks. The Gibson look over the shoulders was edged with the lace, as were the tucked sleeves and collar. It made her feel very feminine and pretty, and she hoped Luke liked it on her.

By the time guests began arriving late in the afternoon, the wind had finally died down to a light breeze, and it promised to be a lovely evening. Trying not to be obvious, Charity mingled with the guests, all the while watching for Luke and his parents to arrive. But some of the young men who'd tried to court her several months before were following her from group to group, and she found it hard to see over their shoulders.

Finally she caught a glimpse of Luke across the room and saw he knew right where she was. She smiled at him, and he began to walk in her direction. She excused herself from the group she'd been talking to and began to head toward Luke. They met in the middle of the room and of one accord they reached out and clasped hands.

"I'm glad you made it. I'd begun to wonder if you'd been sent on another assignment," Charity said.

"The boss knew I was coming here tonight and realizes any party your father hosts is bound to have someone newsworthy in attendance."

"And is that why you are here? To get a story?" Charity couldn't believe how brazen she sounded. But she needed to know.

"I've already got a story written to send in. I came because you are here, and I didn't want to go another minute without seeing you."

His words melted her heart and flooded her being with warmth, and she knew they could have just as easily come from her lips. She smiled and let him draw her hand through his arm, as if he was telling all the young men who'd been following her up until he arrived to look elsewhere. In the past she would have put a man in his place for assuming she might want to be by his side for the rest of the evening. But tonight, her heart soared because Luke claimed her attention in a way that sent prospective beaus in another direction.

They went to speak to their parents and Grammy Rose, who was enjoying all the festivities they'd helped her mother plan. There were games out on the lawn, parlor games inside, and food everywhere. Charity and Luke filled their plates and took them out onto the terrace. The lanterns cast a soft glow, people came and went, but Charity had eyes for no one but Luke. Something seemed different about Luke tonight; he seemed determined—as if he was a man on a mission of some kind.

❧

It was this weekend or never, Luke had decided on the way to the city. But sitting across from Charity on her parents' terrace, he thought he might be losing his nerve to bring the subject up at all. She looked beautiful, dressed in a green gown that brought out the color of her eyes and stood in contrast to her luscious cloud of red hair. How could he possibly think she could give him the time of day, much less her heart?

Yet she'd chosen to spend the evening with him instead of any of those young men who'd been surrounding her, hanging on her every word when he arrived. And they were still there, just waiting for her to give them a sign of any kind to rescue her from him. He'd seen one or two walk by since they'd sat down, but Charity hadn't seemed to notice them. He hoped that meant he did have a chance after all.

"You seem a little. . .distracted tonight, Luke. Is anything wrong?" Charity asked.

"Wrong? How could anything possibly be wrong when I'm sharing a meal with the most beautiful woman here?"

Her laughter tinkled across the table and tumbled into his heart. "Oh, Luke, thank you, but don't you think you're going a little. . .overboard?"

"By saying you are the most beautiful woman here? No." In the lamplight, her eyes seemed to deepen to the green-blue he loved. What caused them to change to that color?

"Well, you are silly then, because there are many women here much prettier than I. But I thank you for the compliment."

"You're welcome." He gazed out over the grounds where

lights along the walkways had just been turned on. "Oh, how nice. Would you walk with me and show me the grounds?"

"Certainly." Charity pushed back her chair and stood. Luke joined her, and she led him to the steps leading from the terrace to the grounds. Once they were on the path made of flat rocks, she took the arm Luke offered her, and they began their stroll. "I love it here at night. Mama wanted the path down to the creek lit, and Papa designed it to have lampposts placed here and there to light the way. You know he wired the boardinghouse for electricity before it ever came to Guthrie. He always thinks ahead."

"He's a brilliant designer. I love the way he placed benches along the way in amongst the rose bushes. My father and mother are so thrilled with the plans he's drawn up for them, and now that the house is being built, I can see why they are so happy."

"His goal has always been to make his clients happy."

They walked along the path until it came to a fork. "Which way do we go?"

"That path circles back to the house, and this one leads down to the creek. Which way do you want to go?"

"You choose." He didn't care which way they went as long as they were together.

"Have you seen the creek? I love it there. Papa has placed several benches down there, too."

"I'd like to see it." When they reached the creek, Luke could see why Charity liked it so much. The water bubbling and babbling over the rocks made a delightful sound, and the moonlight, along with the lamplight reflecting off the water, lit the way to the benches under the trees.

Charity took a seat, and Luke sat down beside her. For the first time since they'd driven into the city, they were alone. He wondered what she would do if he pulled her into his arms just then.

"Well, what do you think of the grounds so far?"

"They are almost as lovely as you are." He reached out and touched her cheek, turning her face so he could look into her eyes. It was now or never. "Charity. . .I. . ."

Even in the darkness, with the light of the moon and the help of the lamps, he could see her eyes darken as he lifted her chin and dipped his head toward her. She didn't move, and he quickly closed the space between them, lightly touching his lips to hers.

He heard her small intake of breath and then. . .felt her lips respond to his. His arms went around her, and he deepened the kiss. His heart felt near to bursting as she kissed him back.

But suddenly she pushed out of his arms and jumped up so quickly he nearly lost his balance. "I. . .I think we should go back to the house now."

"I'm sorry, Charity. I—"

She shook her head. "It's me, I—" She turned and took off back down the path.

"Charity, wait." Luke hurried to reach her, grasped her arm, and pulled her hand through his. "I'll see you safely back. I promise."

As soon as they reached the terrace Charity turned to him and looked so distressed, he groaned inwardly. It appeared he'd done more harm than good to their relationship with his kiss.

She turned to go but Luke stayed her by putting a hand on her forearm. "Please, Charity. Forgive me. I didn't mean to upset you. All I've been trying to do is tell you. . .I've fallen in love with you and I—"

"Oh Luke, please—" she shook her head. "I'm sorry I—it's not you. It's me. I don't know how I feel about anything at this moment. Please forgive *me*." She pulled out of his hold and rushed into the house, leaving him wondering if he'd made the mistake of his life in thinking she might return his feelings. *Dear Lord, please help me to know what to do now.*

❧

Charity was thankful for all the relatives who were staying the night, making it impossible for her and her parents to have their normal after-party discussion. Once she got to her room, all she could do was cry, and she didn't want anyone witnessing her misery—least of all them.

On the one hand, her heart filled with joy over Luke's declaration of love, and on the other, she was filled with confusion over what to do about it. She loved him. She knew she did, and she'd wanted to tell him she felt the same way. But fear that she couldn't be the wife he needed or that he wasn't the man she now believed him to be paralyzed her. She was petrified of making the wrong decision, and she simply didn't know what to do.

She tossed and turned all night and the next morning. Charity was sick at heart. When she didn't come down to breakfast, her mother wasted no time in coming to see what was wrong, and when she didn't return right away, her father evidently decided he'd better find out what was going on, too.

"Maybe I ate something that didn't agree with me. I'm sure

I'll feel better after a while." Charity was sure her red-rimmed eyes didn't fool her parents for a minute, but they didn't press her.

"Will you be all right to stay home by yourself? You won't really be alone. Cook is in the kitchen, of course. I'll have her bring you some tea and toast a little later."

"Thank you, Mama."

A worried frown graced her father's forehead. "You just try to rest, dear. We'll check on you as soon as we get home."

Charity couldn't remember the last time she'd missed church, and she felt awful about doing so now. But she simply couldn't face Luke again so soon after last night. She reached for the Bible on her bedside table and flipped it open. Her gaze fell on Proverbs 3:5 and she read, "Trust in the Lord with all thine heart; and lean not unto thine own understanding." It seemed the perfect verse, for she didn't understand herself at all. But she prayed the Lord would help her to know what to do about Luke and about how she felt about him and help her to know if they could have a future.

She felt a little better by the time her parents got home and came to check on her.

"Luke Johnson asked about you this morning, dear. Did something happen last night we should know about?" her mother asked.

"I. . ." Charity had never been good about trying to hide anything from her parents, and she wasn't going to start now. "Luke told me he loves me last night, and I ran away." Suddenly realizing how much she might have hurt him, she began to cry again. "I don't know how he could love someone like me, who is so afraid to make the wrong decision where he is concerned that I ran away from making any decision at all."

"How *do* you feel about him, Charity?" Her father sat down in the chair beside her bed.

"I love him, too. But Papa, I'm afraid. What if he's not the man I think he is? What if I can't trust him to be the kind of man you and Uncle Ben are?"

"Charity, you've got to stop comparing Luke to your uncle and me. He could well turn out to be a better man than either of us. All your uncle Ben and I have done is try to do the Lord's will in our lives, and I think Luke Johnson is trying to do the very same thing."

"Charity dear, I fear we've spoiled you a bit too much." Her mother sat down on the bed beside her and took hold of her hand. "I'm sure I'm to blame for most of it. I thought I'd never be able to have a child, and when you came along, I—"

"No, it wasn't all you, Faith. We've both been much too indulgent with Charity. I have to take part of the blame," Charity's father said. "We thought we were showing you how to trust, how to make decisions, how to look to the Lord to help with the decisions you make by the way we've lived our lives."

"But perhaps we weren't talking enough about how to go about doing it," her mother added. "If that's the case, I'm sorry. For I thought we taught you to put your life, your future in the Lord's hands. To go to Him when you need guidance instead of. . .thinking you had all the answers yourself."

Her mother's words stung, but Charity knew she'd been spoiled. And she did have the view she didn't need anyone to tell her what to do. . .until recently, anyway. Now she knew she needed direction about as much as anyone could.

"Charity, if you are ever to be truly happy, you have to give control over your life to the Lord. You have to truly seek His guidance. As for what kind of man you need in your life, you need one who puts the Lord first, just as you should be doing. And he needs to put you next in his life, just as you should put him. I think Luke Johnson is that kind of man. If you still have any doubts, then I suggest you take your concerns to the Lord and ask Him to make things clear to you."

Charity nodded. "You're both right. I—" She sniffed, ashamed she wasn't nearly as mature and grownup as she'd always thought she was.

"Do you think you'll be able to come down to Sunday dinner? Or do you want me to have something sent up to you?" her mother asked.

"Please just send something up, Mama. I promise I'll be down for supper."

Both of her parents hugged her, and Charity knew they only wanted the best for her. As they left the room, she realized everything they'd said was true. She was spoiled and stubborn, thinking she knew so much and could handle anything that came her way. Except of course she didn't and couldn't—not alone. She'd been leaning on her own understanding, making decisions without first taking them to the Lord.

The knowledge that she really hadn't been giving her concerns to Him or been asking for His guidance broke her heart, and she got out of bed and down on her knees. "Dear Lord, I am so sorry I've not come to You for guidance and direction in my life. Please forgive me, and please show me if I've been wrong about being afraid to put my trust in Luke. Please help me to know if he is the right man for me, and if I can be the kind of wife he needs. I do love him, Lord, with all my heart, but You already know that. Please just help me to give control over to You and to trust You will show me what You'd have me do. In Jesus' name, Amen."

fifteen

All day Sunday, Luke struggled with what to do about Charity. Had he ruined things between them? She wasn't at church, and he felt responsible even though her parents greeted him and his parents as warmly as ever. He felt even worse when he realized they probably didn't know he'd upset her the evening before.

The next day was Decoration Day, and Luke had never been more confused in his life. He really believed Charity cared for him, and her response to his kiss did nothing to dissuade him. But given that she wasn't ready to hear how he felt or to tell him how she felt about him, told him he'd moved much too quickly. And now he didn't know what to do. They'd planned on driving back to Guthrie together, but would she ride back with him now? Or speak to him if he called her?

He tried to throw off his worry so his parents could have a good day as they headed to the North Canadian River for a picnic. But doing so was easier said than done when they ran into the Logans and their entire family picnicking there, too. They invited Luke and his family to join them.

He spotted Charity helping set dishes out, and he was glad she felt well enough to join her family. He wasn't sure how she would react when she saw him, and he tried not to draw attention to himself as he talked to the men waiting to be called to eat.

But he couldn't keep himself from glancing her way. As usual she looked wonderful, but there seemed to be a shadow under her eyes, as if she hadn't slept well or still felt bad. She must have felt his gaze on her for she turned and looked until she saw him. Then she began to walk toward him. He met her halfway. If she was angry with him, he deserved it, and he'd listen to whatever she wanted to say to him. All he wanted at the moment was to be able to talk to her again. But when they reached each other, she actually smiled.

"Charity, I. . . You weren't at church yesterday. Are you feeling better? I'm sorry if I caused you to—"

"Luke, please don't apologize. I'm the one who—" She stopped, took a deep breath, and then released it. "I'm sorry I ran away the other night. I just. . ." She shook her head and looked up at him, her eyes the deep color he loved. "I'm praying about everything."

"Could we fix a plate and go eat together? Down by the river, so there aren't so many ears?"

Charity turned to see what he did. Members of both families trying hard not to let them know they were watching every move he and Charity made. She surprised him with a chuckle. "Yes, please."

They got in line with the others and made their plates, then ambled off together after Charity grabbed a picnic blanket for them to sit on.

They found a shady spot, spread out the blanket, then sat down to their meal. Luke said a blessing and they began to eat, but he noticed Charity pushed the food around on her plate instead of eating. He set his plate aside. He wasn't very hungry himself.

"Can you tell me what is bothering you so much? What is it I've done to make you so uncertain—"

"I'm not sure we are right for each other, no matter how much I may care about you or you me, Luke. I don't know how you feel about the capital being moved. I don't know whose side you are on in that battle. I've seen you talking to those I know want it moved, and I—I know maybe it shouldn't matter, but it does to me."

"Oh Charity, at first I didn't see the big deal about where the capital was located. But now I've been living in Guthrie and have seen how much it means to everyone there, to you and your family. I can see why it should stay where it is, and that's what I want, too. But I have to be honest with you and tell you I just don't see how it can. Oklahoma City is so much larger, and I can't see how Guthrie could get all the votes needed. I'm sorry."

"And you aren't on the other side?"

Luke chuckled and shook his head. "I'm not. But I do have to talk to people on both sides. I want to report fairly and try not to show where I stand. I think that's the only way I can be the kind of reporter the Lord wants me to be." He paused. Was it was time to tell her? No. He wanted her to love him for who he was. Not because he worked for one paper or another.

"That brings me to the other thing. You know Papa is considering running for governor. If. . .I. . .he. . ."

"Charity, if you are trying to tell me about your father's past. . ."

She inhaled sharply and nodded, her eyes filled with tears as she waited for him to continue.

"There's no need. I know. I've known for a while, and I'd never use the information to hurt you or your family. Never."

She seemed to stifle a sob. "Thank you. It shouldn't bother me, and I'm ashamed it does. But I—it's not just any embarrassment it might cause me. More important than me—I don't want my father hurt again either, and. . ."

Luke reached out and gently touched her lips. "It's all right. I know how much you love your father. And if his past comes out again, it won't be me letting it out. I promise you that, Charity."

"Thank you."

Luke lifted her chin to look into her eyes. They were turning that blue color he'd finally come to realize happened when she was emotional about anything. "Charity, there is more to your response last night than whether I'm on one side or the other in the capital fight. And more even than if I would bring up something in your father's past if he should run, isn't there? I think you are using those as excuses not to trust your heart to me. I think trusting me is what you are really afraid of. But only you know for sure."

She looked down at the fingers she was twisting. "Oh, Luke. I'm not sure I can be the wife you'd want and expect. I've been spoiled all my life, and I'm headstrong—doing things my way before I give them over to the Lord. I want to change, but I don't know how successful I'll be at it. And I want a family, but I also want to design homes for my father's company—although I could probably do that in a home office. I want to be a submissive wife like the Bible says I should be, but I—"

"Charity, all I can tell you is that I love you with all of my heart. And I'm willing to trust it to you. I hope one day you'll be able to trust yours to me." He loved this woman, and he felt sure she loved him, too. But she'd been so honest with him; Luke knew he must tell her what he'd done.

Charity's eyes filled with tears again, and she opened her mouth to speak, but Luke gently touched her lips with his fingertips and shook his head. "There is something I have to tell you, and I'm not doing it to try to sway the way you feel about me. I'm doing it because you deserve the same kind of honesty you've just shown me. I don't work for the *Daily Leader* anymore. I quit on Friday, and Greer hired me that same afternoon. I did it because I couldn't continue working for the paper's owners when I hold such an opposite view of what should be done about the capital."

"Luke. . ."

Luke shook his head and said, "Don't try to give me an answer now. Please just think about it, pray about it, and know that I'm here when you know for sure what it is you want."

&

Charity didn't ride home with Luke. Instead she stayed in the city with her mother and grandmother while her father was on the road trying to drum up as many votes as he could for keeping the capital in Guthrie.

By the time she got back to Guthrie, it was to find that Greer had sent Luke out to try to find out which way the vote would go in many of the other cities around the state. She missed him with every fiber of her being, and she wanted to tell him so, but now wasn't the time. Too much was happening. His career depended on him doing his job—especially now that he had a new one—without being distracted. What she did know without a doubt was she loved Luke and wanted only the best for him. But could she be the woman he needed?

Even though the days seemed to crawl with Luke gone, June 11th came entirely too quickly. She hurried down to the kitchen to help Hope with breakfast. But when she took the biscuits in to the dining room, she nearly dropped them. Luke sat in his usual seat next to hers as if he'd never been gone.

"Good morning." He smiled the smile that reached right into her heart and made her breathless.

Now it soared at the look in his eyes. He was glad to see her. "You're back."

"I am." He smiled. "I returned late last night. I came to cast my vote for Guthrie. You'd never let me forget it if I didn't."

His teasing tone put her at ease. "You're right. I wouldn't."

Hope brought in the bacon and eggs and set them on the table before taking her seat.

"Let's pray," Thomas said. "Dear Lord, we thank You for this day, and we ask for it to be a good one for this town. We ask for Guthrie to win this vote we are about to have, if it be Your will. If Guthrie loses, we ask You to be with us all, to help this town deal with it, and to turn to You when times get hard. We thank You for being with us no matter what the outcome. And we thank You for the food we are about to eat. In Jesus' name we pray, amen."

No one tarried long over breakfast as everyone was eager to go cast their vote. The voting precinct wasn't far away, and they all walked together. The lines were long, giving Charity hope Luke might be wrong about the city winning.

Once they cast their votes, Luke walked her out of the building. "It is so good to see you. I want so badly to talk to you, to see how you are doing. But Greer expects me at the paper. I—"

"We'll have time to talk when the vote is in, Luke. I know you have a job to do. I'm just glad you're home."

"So am I." He looked as if he wanted to say more but then gave a short nod. "I'll see you later."

"See you later."

He turned and headed in one direction while she joined the others to go back to the boardinghouse. It promised to be a very long day.

❧

In midafternoon Charity's parents drove up with Grammy Rose. She'd insisted on casting her vote, too, and they'd come from letting her do just that.

"The lines are long, and that gives me hope," her father said. "But I have to admit they were long in the city, too. I'm glad to be here, though. It seems fitting we be here to find out the outcome—no matter what it is."

Charity was glad they were there, too. It helped the time go by to get Grammy Rose settled back in the house. Her mother was doing much better, and Grammy was ready to be home. Her parents planned to stay several days, and it felt like a family reunion, although they'd all seen each other just over a week before. But as the afternoon turned to evening, it became harder to keep their minds off of the election.

The women all tried to help as they put together a meal. "I love this range," Charity's mother said as she pulled out the pie she'd made from the fresh peaches Ben and Sam had brought in. "As old as it is, it still cooks the same as the first day I used it."

The golden-crusted pie proved it did, as did the pot roast Hope served along with potatoes and carrots. "You're right. I hope it lasts another ten years at least."

Luke didn't make it back in time for supper, but everyone knew he'd manage to get news to them as soon as he knew for sure what the returns were showing, and Hope kept a plate warm for when he arrived.

They kept busy after dinner by playing parlor games and putting together a puzzle or two with Hope's children, who were given permission to stay up until they knew the election results. It was just after ten o'clock when Luke came in the front door. Charity could tell by the look in his face it wasn't good news. "I'm sorry everyone. It looks like Oklahoma City is going to become the capital." His gaze met Charity's, and he shook his head. "I wish I came bearing better news."

"It's not your fault, Luke. Come on into the kitchen. Hope has kept supper warm for you," Charity said. Her heart ached because it'd taken her so long to realize how much Luke cared about her and her family. His concern was very real, and he looked as sad as everyone else.

The other boarders made their way up to their rooms, and Hope sent her children to bed. The rest of the family joined Luke at the kitchen table while he ate and gave them the latest numbers. "It was pretty obvious early on that Guthrie would lose, but I kept hoping some of the later returns would turn it around. Greer is almost beside himself."

"I imagine so. He fought tooth and nail to keep the capital

here, but I don't think it's going to comfort him any. He and Niblack have been at it for months now," Charity's father said.

"It's probably a good thing Niblack went to Tulsa to wait for the returns. I don't think it would be good for those two men to be in the same town tonight," Uncle Ben said.

"Well, stewing about it all isn't going to do us any good. We've got to turn it all over to the Lord and let Him help us deal with the results of this election," Charity's father said.

"You're right. It's all we can do. I've got to go back to the paper to help put out tomorrow's copy." Luke yawned. "I'm hoping we get through before midnight. Thanks for saving supper for me, Hope."

"You're welcome. See you tomorrow."

Charity followed Luke to the door. "Thank you for bringing us the news in person."

"I couldn't let you just read about it in the morning. I am so sorry—"

Charity looked up at him and saw the sincerity in his eyes. "I know. And I realize it wasn't easy to come tell us. But Papa is right. All we can do now is take it to the Lord."

"That's right." Luke reached out and tucked an errant curl behind her ear. For a moment, Charity thought he might kiss her, wanted him to, but he gave a little shake of his head and turned to go. "I'll see you in the morning. Good night."

"'Night, Luke." Charity watched him hurry down the walk, knowing that she wouldn't sleep a wink until she heard his footsteps on the stairs and knew he was safely back home.

And as soon as she could, she was determined to tell him she'd decided that with the Lord's help she *would* be the kind of woman he needed. He'd proved to her in so many ways what kind of man he was, and she couldn't wait to tell him she loved him with all her heart. But it would have to wait until the timing was right, and she would trust the Lord to let her know when it was.

❧

A somber group set out for church the next morning, but the lesson Preacher Bradley gave lifted them all up and reminded them that, while the future of Guthrie would hold disappointment and hardship for many, it was only a passing thing.

"Our focus is on the hereafter and getting to heaven." Preacher Bradley drove his message home. "The Lord will see us through this deep disappointment we're experiencing now, and we'll all go on with our lives, looking toward a much better home in heaven for all eternity, with no worries about it ever being taken away."

By the time they left church, Charity felt uplifted, and from the looks of her family, they all did, too. Luke fell into step with her, and even he looked better than the night before.

"What a good lesson today. Life is going to give us disappointments. But we have a hope for the future, forever through Christ. It's time to try to put the election in perspective. We can't change it, but we can try to accept it with grace and go on. Wherever that takes us," Grammy Rose said. "We're blessed in many ways. And Guthrie may not be the capital after last night, but it will always be home to me."

They'd all decided the night before to have Sunday dinner out, and they went to one of their favorite places, the Miller

Café. It'd been there since the beginning days, only the Miller children ran it now, with Mr. and Mrs. Miller visiting with the guests now and again. They were treated like family as they were seated at a huge round table. Aunt Samantha had worked at the restaurant when she'd first come to Guthrie, and Charity's Uncle Ben recounted how afraid he was some handsome cowboy would win her heart before he had a chance to.

They were served fried chicken, mashed potatoes, and gravy all family style, and it appeared everyone thoroughly enjoyed the meal. Afterward, Luke asked Charity if she'd like to take a walk with him, and she didn't hesitate. "Yes, I would."

They took their leave before everyone else was ready to go, and Charity felt sure they'd be the topic of conversation for the rest of the afternoon. But she didn't mind. She thought they were going to the creek, but instead Luke led her to the bench in the backyard of the boardinghouse.

"They won't think to look for us here, and this way we can have some privacy. Besides, Cottonwood Creek will be overflowing with people today."

Charity's heart felt all fluttery as she realized he wanted to be alone with her. Luke waited until she sat down and then joined her on the bench.

He was quiet for a few moments, and then he turned and took both her hands in his, looking her in the eyes. "Charity, I don't know what else I can do to prove I love you. I do— with all my heart. But I need to know: do you think you can ever learn to love me, to trust me to love you forever?"

Charity blinked back the sudden tears of happiness that

threatened. "Oh Luke, I've loved you for weeks now. I've just been afraid to let myself trust what I knew to be true—I think because in doing so, I'd be giving up control over my future. But I know how wrong I've been, and I've learned I *should* be giving control over my life to the Lord, looking to Him to guide me in my decisions instead of relying on myself. I'm sorry for hurting you by running away the other night, by not admitting then how much I love you."

"Who are you relying on now, Charity?"

"I'm relying on the Lord. I've given it all over to Him, and He's shown me you are the man I love and the one who loves me the way I need to be loved. I know I can trust you with my heart for the rest of our lives—if you're still sure. . ."

Luke pulled her into his arms and gathered her close. "Oh Charity, I'm more convinced than ever we're meant to be together. The sun might be setting on Guthrie's future, but it's just beginning to rise for ours—if you'll marry me. I promise you I will love you more with each and every sunrise and sunset we share for the rest of our lives." Luke didn't wait for her answer before his lips captured hers in a kiss intended to convince her he meant every word he'd said.

As Charity responded, the total joy of knowing this man loved her washed over her, convincing her she'd finally let the Lord show her the way. She broke the kiss only to say, "I love you Luke. I'll be honored to become Mrs. Luke Johnson and share the rest of our lives together."

Their lips met once again, sealing their promise to one another—until the sound of several automobiles approaching the drive drew them apart. It was time to tell the family. . .as if they needed to be told.

epilogue

The next few weeks were a mixture of utter sadness and total joy. There was no way Guthrie could have won with 31,301 votes to Oklahoma City's 96,261. Even if Guthrie had received all of Shawnee's votes, the 8,382 wouldn't have come close to helping. But on top of losing the vote, the governor added insult to injury. He didn't even wait until the final vote results were in before he sent his people into his office to retrieve the seal of the state and meet him in Oklahoma City to set up the government in a hotel there.

Outrage resonated across the state as the *Oklahoma State Capitol's* headlines proclaimed, CAPITAL OF THE STATE RAVISHED BY BRIGANDS FROM THE SOUTH. Citizens in Guthrie remained in shock, and Guthrie boosters vowed to sue to have the capital restored to the city. Much as he wished otherwise, even Charity's father knew there was no chance of them winning, and his name was already out there as a possible candidate in the next election.

But along with all the frustration and sadness Charity's family felt over Guthrie's loss of the capital, they were rejoicing for another reason altogether. Charity and Luke had set a wedding date for the middle of July, and it couldn't come fast enough for either of them.

Still, it was a busy month. Charity and Luke attended Lizzy's wedding as a newly engaged couple. The Logans presented Lizzy and Edward with the house plans Charity had worked on so hard, and included an offer of a very good deal from her father to build the house when they were ready.

"You will design our home, won't you?" Luke had asked Charity.

"Of course I will, with your input. Where do you want to make our home: here or in the city?"

"It's up to you, of course, my love. I don't think I'll have a job here much longer if the lawsuit to keep the capital in Guthrie is lost. Mr. Greer has said he will leave Guthrie if that happens. I've already been offered a position with several papers in the city, but we'll live wherever you want," he answered.

Charity knew she'd found the man she needed. Luke put the Lord first in his life and her next. He'd even been willing to give up his dream for her. She found it much easier than she'd ever thought it would be to say, "Guthrie will always be my hometown, Luke, and I can come back anytime. But I'll go wherever you feel is best for your career. I can be happy anywhere as long as we are together. If working in the city is what will be best for you, then I look forward to building a future with you in the new capital."

Luke had pulled her into his arms for a kiss. "I love you, Charity Logan. I can't wait to make you my wife."

Now they stood exchanging vows on the terrace at her parents' home in Oklahoma City, in front of family and friends: both sets of parents, of course, Charity's aunt and uncle, Hope and Matt and their families, and Grammy Rose. Even Lizzy and her new husband just back from a wedding trip to Eureka Springs made it. So many who meant so much to Charity and Luke were there to witness the happiest day of their lives.

"I pronounce you man and wife," Minister Bradley pronounced. "You may kiss your bride."

Charity stood on tiptoe as Luke whispered in her ear, "I love you, my wife," just before his lips claimed hers. The sun set over the creek as they turned to greet family and friends as Mr. and Mrs. Luke Johnson.

A Letter To Our Readers

Dear Reader:

In order that we might better contribute to your reading enjoyment, we would appreciate your taking a few minutes to respond to the following questions. We welcome your comments and read each form and letter we receive. When completed, please return to the following:

Fiction Editor
Heartsong Presents
PO Box 719
Uhrichsville, Ohio 44683

1. Did you enjoy reading *Sooner Sunset* by Janet Lee Barton?
   ❏ Very much! I would like to see more books by this author!
   ❏ Moderately. I would have enjoyed it more if

   _____

   _____

   _____

2. Are you a member of **Heartsong Presents**? ❏ Yes ❏ No
   If no, where did you purchase this book? _____

   _____

3. How would you rate, on a scale from 1 (poor) to 5 (superior), the cover design? _____

4. On a scale from 1 (poor) to 10 (superior), please rate the following elements.

   _____ Heroine   _____ Plot
   _____ Hero   _____ Inspirational theme
   _____ Setting   _____ Secondary characters

5. These characters were special because? _____

_____

_____

6. How has this book inspired your life? _____

_____

_____

7. What settings would you like to see covered in future
   Heartsong Presents books? _____

_____

_____

8. What are some inspirational themes you would like to see
   treated in future books? _____

_____

_____

9. Would you be interested in reading other **Heartsong
   Presents** titles? ❏ Yes ❏ No

10. Please check your age range:

    ❏ Under 18   ❏ 18-24

    ❏ 25-34   ❏ 35-45

    ❏ 46-55   ❏ Over 55

Name _____

Occupation _____

Address _____

City, State, Zip _____

E-mail _____

When they reached the creek, Luke could see why Charity liked it so much.

The water bubbling and babbling over the rocks made a delightful sound, and the moonlight, along with the lamplight reflecting off the water, lit the way to the benches under the trees.

Charity took a seat, and Luke sat down beside her. For the first time since they'd driven into the city, they were alone. He wondered what she would do if he pulled her into his arms just then.

"Well, what do you think of the grounds so far?"

"They are almost as lovely as you are." He reached out and touched her cheek, turning her face so he could look into her eyes. It was now or never. "Charity. . .I. . ."

Even in the darkness, with the light of the moon and the help of the lamps, he could see her eyes darken as he lifted her chin and dipped his head toward her. She didn't move, and he quickly closed the space between them, lightly touching his lips to hers.

He heard her small intake of breath and then. . .felt her lips respond to his. His arms went around her, and he deepened the kiss. His heart felt near to bursting as she kissed him back.

But suddenly she pushed out of his arms and jumped up so quickly he nearly lost his balance. "I. . .I think we should go back to the house now."

JANET LEE BARTON has lived all over the southern United States, but she and her husband plan to now stay put in Oklahoma. With three daughters and six grandchildren between them, they feel blessed to have at least one daughter and her family living in the same town. Janet loves being able to share her faith through her writing. Happily married to her very own hero, she is ever thankful that the Lord brought Dan into her life, and she wants to write stories that show that the love between a man and a woman is at its best when the relationship is built with God at the center. She's very happy that the kind of romances the Lord has called her to write can be read by and shared with women of all ages, from teenagers to grandmothers alike.

Books by Janet Lee Barton

HEARTSONG PRESENTS

Don't miss out on any of our super romances. Write to us at the following address for information on our newest releases and club information.

Heartsong Presents Readers' Service
PO Box 721
Uhrichsville, OH 44683

Or visit www.heartsongpresents.com